Liberty Empowered

by

Alicia Dean

Isle of Fangs Book 3

Liberty Empowered

Contact Information: info@thewildrosepress.com

Cover Art by *Lisa Dawn MacDonald*

The Wild Rose Press, Inc.
PO Box 708
Adams Basin, NY 14410-0708
Visit us at www.thewildrosepress.com

Publishing History
First Edition, 2022
Trade Paperback ISBN 978-1-5092-3982-5
Digital ISBN 978-1-5092-3983-2

Previously Self-published
Published in the United States of America

Loud creaking noises rose above the din. Where once there were a horde of bats, at least a few dozen vampires now stood. People tried to flee, but several were grabbed by vampires.

To her left, Trey clutched a terrified, screaming woman. He bit into her neck. Blood poured onto the ground. Liberty fired and hit him in the shoulder. He spun, clutching his arm. The woman fell.

He squinted at Liberty and smiled. She and Trey had had run-ins before. The last time, he'd attacked Hannah and Liberty had fired at him and missed. Not this time…

He stalked toward her, one hand on his bleeding shoulder. She aimed for his heart. Before she could squeeze the trigger, he darted and was no longer in front of her. She searched through the chaos. A shiver rolled over her skin. Not having Trey in her sights made her nervous.

Ryan.

Where was Ryan? She spotted him several feet away, struggling with a female vampire. Ryan was strong, but he was no match for the strength of vampires… even a woman. The heavy-set purple-haired girl sank her fangs into his neck.

Liberty rushed toward them, gun drawn. Before she could reach them, someone grabbed her from behind. She caught a glimpse of Trey from her peripheral. He snatched her up by the shoulders and tossed her in the air. She landed hard on her back. Spots danced in front of her eyes, and her head swam. Darkness squeezed against her vision. Don't pass out, Ryan needs you, don't pass out…

Acknowledgments

I would like to thank my beta reader, Ms. Trace, for not only her awesome suggestions, but for her devotion and love for the series. And thank you to my fabulous critique partners, Krysta Scott and Kathy L Wheeler. I'd be lost without you. Thank you to my daughter, Lacey, for her last minute read-through and helpful suggestions. Lastly, I'd like to thank vampires. If you didn't exist, the world of books and televisions and movies would be a much more boring place.

Chapter 1

Sang Croc Island,
French Polynesia

Hannah Rankin just barely resisted the urge to stomp her foot. Her grandparents already treated her like a child, she couldn't give them any more reason to think of her that way. She was *fourteen years old*, for God's sake.

She crossed her arms tightly over her chest, but managed to keep her feet still. "Please, can't we stay? I don't want to leave Sang Croc."

"Honey, we've been here four months." Her grandmother folded one of Hannah's shirts with the ease born of years of practice and laid it gently in the open suitcase. She glanced at Hannah with a sympathetic smile. "You have to go back and start school."

"Let me go to school here."

"We can't live here. Our home is in Oklahoma." Her grandmother's brow creased. She wrung her hands together. Any kind of conflict made her nervous. Hannah usually didn't argue with her, but this was mega important.

Her grandfather spoke from where he sat on the hotel sofa. "Look, I know you'll miss Liberty. But you can keep in touch on the Facebooks."

His misuse of the word normally amused or annoyed

her. Now, she was too worried for it to do either. Liberty wasn't the reason she wanted to stay. She liked her and would miss her, but the main reason she didn't want to leave was because of the Cave of Youth. Somewhere on this island was a cave that held magical water that restored youth. If she could find it, she could help her grandparents. They'd raised her after her piece of crap mother abandoned her. They were getting old, and she couldn't lose them. God, what would she do if she lost them? Go back to her drugged out mother?

Her throat clogged with tears and this time, she did stomp her foot. "If you make me go, I'll never speak to you again."

Her grandmother's mouth dropped open, and tears welled. Hannah looked away to prevent hurtling into in her arms and begging for forgiveness.

"You apologize right now, young lady." Her grandfather's voice was unusually harsh.

The apology was on the tip of her tongue, but she choked it back. She was *right*, dammit. "No, I will not!" She whirled and ran out of the room, slamming the hut door behind her.

She listened for the sounds of her grandparents following her. Even if they did, they were too old, they'd never catch her.

Her breath heaved in and out. A twinge of guilt surfaced. Her grandparents had been awesome. They loved her. Took care of her. Treated her great. So why was she being such a bitch?

Because… they just wouldn't *listen*. She was only trying to *help* them. Couldn't they see that?

Tears blinded her as she ran down the beach toward the ocean. Maybe she should just dive in and not come back up. She'd rather be dead than end up back with her mother—

A figure appeared from nowhere directly in front of her. She skidded to a halt, barely in time to keep from slamming into him. What the *F*? Her heart thudded. She panted, trying to catch her breath. He was tall— extremely tall—with shaggy dark hair that fell over his forehead and accentuated unusually pale skin.

"Uh, excuse me." She started around him, but he stepped in front of her. She peered up at him, her heart pounding even harder. "I'm sorry. If you could just let me by…" She tried to strengthen her voice, but between the tears, the running, and terror, she didn't succeed.

Something moved in her peripheral vision, and suddenly, there were two more guys with him. One was short and thin, with a goatee and spiked brown hair. The other was almost as tall as the first. His arms were covered in tattoos. They were equally pale-skinned.

"Ah." The first one gave a creepy smile. "Just who we were looking for."

"Looking for?" Her voice came out in a squeak. "Me?" She glanced behind her. Nothing but pure darkness. Would her grandparents come after her? She swallowed and backed away. "I'm sorry, I need to…"

With each step she took, the vampires took one as well, walking slowly toward her.

Panic thrummed through her body, making her knees tremble. She backed away more quickly, preparing to turn and flee, but afraid to take her eyes off them. "If you touch me, I'll scream. My grandparents will hear, and they'll come out."

The first guy chuckled. "Oh yeah, they'll definitely come out. We're counting on it." She barely saw him move, but in an instant, she was plastered against his chest, his arm around her waist, her feet dangling above the ground. She let out a yelp, shoving against him with all her might.

He didn't budge. He lifted an eyebrow, and a slow, chilling grin spread across his face. "So, where's that scream you promised?" He opened his mouth and showed his teeth... not normal teeth... fangs... A... vampire?

Her legs shook. Terror froze her flesh. "Please... oh please..." she whimpered. Her heart vibrated so hard she thought it would explode. He bent his head toward her neck. She let out a blood curdling scream.

****

One week later

An evening breeze blew in from the ocean, lifting and then lowering the target that hung between two coconut palm trees. Liberty Van Helsing drew in a deep breath and focused, repeating her new mantra, *the fewer vampires you kill, the more humans that die.* She *had* to improve as a hunter. Lives depended on it.

She shook out her shoulders, planted her feet in the sand, gripped the butt of the pistol, and narrowed her eyes on the target. She drew in a lungful of ocean air, and—

A hurtling object flashed in her peripheral just before something slammed into her shoulder. She stumbled, the gun went off—and she missed the target completely.

She lifted her upper body and rested on her elbows. "Son of a bitch!" A Frisbee lay on the beach a few feet away. She sprang to her feet, brushing sand off her jeans and whirled on Eli, who leaned nonchalantly against a

4

palm tree. "What the hell?"

He grinned. "A little distraction."

"You threw a *Frisbee* at me? While I was taking aim?"

"Do you think the EO's will wait for you to settle into your stance on a hunt?"

She huffed out a breath. "Maybe not, but you could have given me a head's up."

He pushed off the tree and sauntered toward her, stopping a few inches away, his dark blond hair blowing in the wind like a tarnished halo.

Her breathing slowed, the way it did every time he came near. She squelched the urge to back away. Forcing herself to meet his glittering silver gaze, she lifted her chin.

He tightened his jaw and gritted out, "The Evil Ones aren't going to give you a head's up, Liberty. They're going to come at you, as fast and hard as they can. You have to be ready, for anything. Especially now that Rupert has called off the truce."

She shrugged, doing her best to conceal how terrified she was that the enraged leader of the EO's had a vendetta against her. "Rupert will calm down. He'll give up."

He grunted a disbelieving laugh. "You don't know Rupert. He never gives up."

"Are you afraid of him?"

"I'm not afraid for me. He might make me suffer, but he'll never kill me." A muscle ticked in his jaw, and he looked out toward the water. "But he'll come after you. He'd like nothing more than to hurt someone I lo—" He jerked his gaze back to her with a grimace. "Someone I care about."

Love? Had he been about to say he *loved* her?

No, and even if he was, what did it matter? She didn't feel that way about him. She was a vampire hunter. She couldn't feel that way about a vampire.

"Speaking of Rupert…"

Eli edged back, eyes wary. "Yeah?"

"Aren't we going to talk about his being your father? About what happened between you two?"

"Nothing to talk about. He's my father, a fact I'd rather forget, end of story."

"How did you wind up defecting from the Evil Ones?"

"It's a long story."

"We have plenty of time."

"No, we don't. We need to use our time wisely, so we don't have to send you back to Oklahoma in a body bag."

"A body bag?"

"Yeah, you know, because you're such a lousy shot."

Her hackles rose. "I'm not a lousy shot."

"You had, what, half a dozen chances at Trey, and still missed his heart?"

Her shoulders fell. He was right. Trey was an unstable, vicious vampire and she'd barely escaped his attacks more than once. She might have learned a lot since coming to Sang Croc from Oklahoma—how to shoot a bow, how to fight—but she couldn't hit the broad side of a hut with her gun. She let out an exasperated breath. "Face it, I'll never be the hunter my father was."

"No, you won't. But you don't have to be a complete failure. The full moon is a week away. You have to be ready by then."

She crossed her arms over her chest and frowned. "It's my birthday," she blurted, then immediately wished she could take it back.

"What's your birthday?"

She dropped her arms, exasperated with herself for sounding like a petulant child. "On the full moon night, next Sunday. It's my nineteenth birthday." And the first one she'd spend without her mother. She hadn't seen her in four months. It seemed like a lifetime. An ache filled her chest, and she drew in a shuddering breath. She missed her so much.

"So."

Liberty lifted her brows. "*So*?"

He shrugged. "It's just a birthday. If you don't want it to be your last, we better get back to training."

Asshole. She tightened her lips and glanced down the beach where the unharmed target hung, silhouetted by the golden pink dusk that hovered above the water.

"Maybe Ryan will care, even if you don't."

He chuckled. "Are you trying to make me jealous?"

Was she? She hoped not. She didn't want to be *that* girl. Besides, she and Ryan weren't even together, at least not like a couple. But Ryan was so much more *caring* than Eli.

"No, I'm not trying to make you jealous. Just pointing out that Ryan is much nicer to me than you are."

"Nice never stopped a raging group of vampires." He picked the gun up and thrust it toward her. "Now, shoot."

She snatched it from his hand, whirled to the target, lifted the gun, and squeezed the trigger. A hole blasted through the silhouette, just to the left of center. Excitement zipped through her, and she turned back to

Eli with a smile. "I did it! That was good, right?"

He grinned. "Yeah, that was good." He took her shoulders and twisted her body to face the target. "Now, do it again."

Two hours later, after she'd practiced until she thought her arms would fall off, she began to see improvement. She wasn't where she needed to be, but if she practiced every night until the hunt, maybe she would survive.

"Okay, now for the last part of your lesson." Eli took hold of her shoulders and gently kneaded them. As always, she marveled at how his cool vampire flesh could incite a heated rush through her veins with one little touch. She pushed back those thoughts. Eli was off limits for many reasons. Not only was he a vampire and she a hunter, he was unpredictable, always seemed on the verge of doing something rash, something with fatal consequences. Besides, he'd made it clear they could never be together. It was her duty to carry on the Van Helsing name, and she couldn't do that if she hooked up with a vampire.

"What are we doing?" She could barely manage a choked whisper over the lump in her throat. Damn... why did his nearness make her insides quiver?

"If you want to be a successful hunter, you'll have to tap into the speed and strength of the Van Helsing lineage."

"I keep hearing that, but I don't know how."

"I'm going to help. Close your eyes."

Her eyes drifted shut. A small shudder quivered through her.

"Feel the blood coursing through your veins." Deep, husky tones washed over her skin. "In your blood, there is power."

"But I don't know how to—"

"Shhh, don't talk. Just feel."

She took a slow deep breath of salty air. In the distance, ocean waves lapped on the shore and sea gulls squawked. Eli was so near, she could hear his heart beating. How did he expect her to focus when he was so… close? She swallowed loudly, pushing aside thoughts of Eli.

Focus…

Concentrating on the blood rushing through her veins, she made the effort to feel instead of think. The energy. The power. In that blood was the Van Helsing gene. Her father and his father before him, all had the power, the speed and strength of the Van Helsings. She may not have known her father long, but she was still his child… a Van Helsing.

Strong, fast, a hunter…

Nothing. Not a hint of the elusive Van Helsing power. She grunted in frustration and opened her eyes. "I can't do it."

Eli gripped her arms. "You *can*. You're a Van Helsing."

"Yeah, well I only found that out four months ago, and so far, I don't *feel* like a Van Helsing."

"You've been on three successful hunts."

"Yes. I killed a few vampires. Fortunately, I only ran into a few. What is going to happen when I'm face to face with a group of them? I'm toast, that's what."

"If you think you are, then you are."

She twisted away from him and let out an irritated sigh. "Thanks for that bit of insight, oh wise one."

He gave a small mock bow. "Any time."

"Listen, I'm going to call it a night." She brushed wayward strands of hair back from her face. "This is useless."

He shook his head. "If you give up that easily, you'll never become the hunter you need to be."

"I could practice twenty-four/seven for the rest of my life, and I still will never be the hunter I need to be."

He growled and opened his mouth to speak, then snapped it shut and whirled toward the tree line. Liberty followed his gaze. She didn't hear anything, didn't see—

A figure burst from the trees, running straight for them. Liberty lunged for her gun, one knee in the sand. She took aim, finger tensed on the trigger. A few yards away, a young girl swayed, eyes wild and darting from side to side. Her blood-soaked blouse hung in tatters on her thin frame.

Chapter 2

Sickness wound through Liberty's stomach. "Hannah!" She dropped the gun and rushed over. Blood streamed from her neck. Her face was as white as the sand. "What happened?"

Hannah's unfocused gaze lifted to Liberty, and she slumped toward the ground. Eli appeared beside them like a flash, caught her, and eased her to the sand.

Liberty dropped to her knees and took hold of Hannah's shoulder. "Hannah? Can you hear me?"

Eli stood, looking into the trees. "Where did she come from? What was she doing out there?"

"I don't know, but she's in bad shape. I need to help her." The blood on Hannah's neck was dark and sticky in the meager moonlight. Bile pinched the inside of Liberty's cheek, and her limbs shook. She averted her gaze from the vile liquid, trying to block the rusty, nauseating scent.

"Liberty." Eli's strained voice came from somewhere above. "You okay? Can you handle the… blood?"

She looked up into his face and cringed. His skin was mottled, gray and tight, his eyes red.

Oh God. He was fighting the urge. Poor Hannah. Her saviors were a hunter with an aversion to blood and a vampire with an uncontrollable lust for it.

"I'm fine." She had to be fine. Blood was a part of

her life now. She dug a vial from her jeans pocket and flipped off the lid. Holding Hannah's head up, Liberty tipped the vial to her lips. "Drink." Hannah frowned, and her eyes drifted shut. A moan left her throat. *Shit*. She was slipping away. Liberty's heart raced. "Come on, please, drink this, or you'll to die."

Hannah didn't open her eyes, but her lips parted. Liberty poured the contents of the vial—her healing Van Helsing blood—into her mouth. The disgusting liquid dribbled between her lips. Liberty shuddered. Forcing her thoughts from the blood, she waited, biting her lip. *Please wake up, Hannah, please...*

Hannah coughed, then groaned and slowly opened her eyes. Color seeped back into her cheeks.

Liberty smoothed the matted blonde hair off Hannah's damp forehead. "How do you feel?"

She winced. "Better." Frowning, she glanced around. "What happened? What am I doing out here?"

"Good question. Once you've rested a few minutes, maybe you'll start to remember." Hopefully the trauma and blood loss were why she couldn't recall, and it wasn't something more long-term. They needed to know what happened so they could protect her—and others on the island.

Liberty glanced over her shoulder at Eli. "We need to get her inside. Your place is closer. Whoever did this could still be out there and could show up any moment."

"I can handle whatever happens. She's fine right here."

Liberty scowled at him. He was such a dick sometimes. How could she have a thing for him? "What if there are several of them? Please, let's get her inside." His house was ten yards away. It only made sense.

He let out a frustrated breath, but scooped Hannah into his arms as if she weighed nothing. She drifted back into unconsciousness. Liberty tried not to worry. She was probably just weak, she'd be okay. She had to be.

Eli carried Hannah, leading the way up the beach to his house.

Just inside the doorway, Liberty halted. A girl paced the living room floor. She was a few years older than Liberty, tall, slender, with long blonde hair. She wore a short, red, sequined dress with matching stilettos. She narrowed her eyes on them, and her gaze dropped to Hannah, still in Eli's arms. Liberty had witnessed that expression way too many times. *Damn...* another vampire.

The girl lunged across the room toward Hannah.

"Angelique, no!" Eli's shout brought her to a stop. She stood, panting, staring at Hannah like a lion stares at a gazelle.

Liberty looked from the girl to Eli. "What the hell?"

Eli grimaced. "My latest apprentice."

Oh shit.

"I turned her on the last full moon. I'm trying to get her... acclimated. And, thanks to you, she'll be my last progeny."

Killing Eli's brother—a murdering, out of control psycho vampire who needed killing—Liberty had eliminated Eli's ability to turn vampires. If a vampire was killed by a Van Helsing, the entire lineage lost their ability to procreate. The good news was, she'd also taken away Rupert's ability to procreate.

This was the first time she'd seen someone Eli turned. An odd mixture of disgust, sympathy, and... jealousy pierced her. Just how intimate was the acclimation? The girl was pretty. Eli was a player. She could do the math.

Disgusted, Liberty gave an inward groan. She'd thought she was through with her childish, unwarranted jealousy after Eli's vampire former lover, Grace, left the island a few weeks earlier, but apparently not.

Angelique's eyes reddened, and the skin on her face creased. "But I'm so… hungry." She licked her lips and extended her fangs. "And look at all that delicious blood."

Eli lowered Hannah to the sofa, then grabbed Angelique's upper arms. Pulling her close, he stared into her face. "Control, remember? This girl is hurt. She's our guest. I'll bring you something to eat later."

His words sent a shiver over Liberty's skin. That 'something to eat' would no doubt be some unsuspecting human. Although, as unlikely as it seemed, some of the humans willingly fed vampires.

Liberty settled on the sofa next to Hannah. Color had come back into her skin, and her eyes drifted open. She rose to a sitting position and looked around the room. "Liberty?" Tears poured down her cheeks, and her body shook. "Oh, God, Liberty."

"It's okay. You're safe now. Tell me what happened."

Unfortunately, Liberty knew, at least a little of it. She'd been attacked by vampires. And not for the first time. Liberty hadn't known Hannah long, but she cared about her. Not only did they share Oklahoma roots, she was a nice kid. Raised an only child, Liberty considered Hannah the sister she'd never had. And, the girl's life had been endangered more than once, because of Liberty. Each previous incident, Hannah had been mesmerized to forget about the attacks, forget she'd seen vampires. Would they be able to continue the ruse?

"Vampires." Hannah's shocked blue gaze latched onto Liberty. "They took us. Vampires. Oh God…"

Dread crept up her spine. "Took us? Us who?"

Her body vibrated more violently. "They have my grandparents." Her wild, frightened gaze swung to Liberty. "I have to help them. I have to go back."

"Back where? Who has them?"

"The Evil Ones." Eli spoke from over Liberty's shoulder.

She glanced at him. "How do you know?" Of course he was right. Who else would it be?

He ignored her, locking his attention on Hannah. "You were held at their compound, weren't you? A blood bag for the EO's?"

"You believe me? You know about… Vampires?" Her stunned whispered filled the room.

Liberty tightened her mouth and met Eli's gaze. She clutched Hannah's hands. "Yes. We know."

Hannah gave a jerky nod. "Y-y-yes. We were used as food for the…" Her breath caught on a sob.

Nausea clenched Liberty's stomach. Rupert had told her—bragged to her—about the humans they kept at the compound for food, but she'd put it out of her mind since she'd been in the midst of a search for a murderer. Now it came back to her, and her heart sank. "Those poor people. Held captive to be fed on and sate those monsters' sadistic desires."

"Some of them are there voluntarily," Eli said. "Most of them are treated well."

Liberty twisted to him in shock. "Don't tell me you're defending this?"

He shrugged. "It's their way of life. They have to live."

"There are options. Animals or willing humans. There's no excuse to keep these people against their will."

Eli shrugged again and said to Hannah, "How did you make it here? The compound is fifteen miles away. You couldn't walk all that distance on your own, not in this condition."

Hannah's blue eyes clouded, and her brow furrowed. "I-I don't know. I can't remember." Her face crumpled, and she sobbed, her shoulders quivering. "My grandparents. I have to help them."

Liberty hugged her. "Shhh, don't worry." Hannah's frame felt like skin and bones. "It will be okay. I promise." Liberty pulled away and brushed hair off Hannah's pale face. "Are you hungry?"

She nodded.

Liberty looked up at Eli. "You have anything to eat?"

He grinned. "Just you two."

Fury spiked her blood, and she gritted her teeth. "Really?" She darted a glance toward Hannah. "Now? Not funny." She gave him one last glare and turned back to Hannah. "I'll take you to my house. You can get something to eat and rest there until we figure out what to do."

"Can I talk to you for a sec?" Eli's expression was calm, but beneath his words, Liberty sensed a hint of anger. Maybe more than a hint. She squeezed Hannah's hand. "I'll be right back."

Liberty followed Eli into the kitchen and leaned her butt against the counter. "Well?"

"I know what you're thinking, and you can get it out of your head right now."

"You don't know what I'm thinking."

"You want to go rescue her grandparents. But you can't do that."

Maybe he *did* know what she was thinking. "Why not?"

"Not only is the compound well-guarded and dangerous, some of the humans are there of their own free will."

"So you said, but her grandparents aren't there voluntarily. I can at least help them."

He threw his hands in the air and let them drop to his sides. "You have to listen to me. You can't rescue her family. You're a hunter, Liberty. Your job is to hunt on full moon nights, not charge off like Wonder Barbie. You are the last of the Van Helsing line. If anything happens to you, what do you think will happen to the people on this island? The Evil Ones will pillage and plunder to their hearts' content."

"Nothing will happen to me."

"I know. Because you're not going."

Liberty barked a laugh. "How do you think you can stop me?"

"You forget, I'm stronger than you. If I have to, I'll handcuff you to me."

She ran her hands through her hair and shook her head. "I need to get Hannah home. We'll talk about this later."

He grabbed her upper arms and captured her eyes with his silver gaze. "Don't do anything stupid. Don't do *anything* without talking to me."

Liberty twisted free and drew in a stuttered breath.

"Fine."

"Promise?"

"I said fine!" She stalked out of the kitchen. She couldn't make any promises. If she could help Hannah's grandparents, she would. Yes, it was risky, but what good was she as a hunter if she couldn't save people she cared about?

****

Liberty drove between the gates of the Van Helsing house and parked in the driveway. Laying her head against the headrest, she released a weary sigh. It had been a long day, and an even longer night. Three a.m., and she'd been up since sunrise. Back home in Oklahoma, she would be snuggled in a cozy bed, her head on a fluffy pillow. Her mother would wake her with a cup of coffee, and they'd share breakfast and girl talk.

A knot of sadness banded her chest. She drew in a deep breath, swallowing back tears. God, she missed her mother. How long would it be before she saw her? Leaving the island was not an option, and no way would she allow her mother to visit. It was too dangerous. Did that mean she might *never* see her again?

Dismissing the depressing thought, she looked at Hannah, dozing in the passenger seat. Poor thing. Liberty hated to wake her, but she couldn't carry her.

Liberty gently shook her shoulder. "Hannah?"

Hannah blinked her eyes open. "Where are we?"

"At my house. Come on, let's get you inside and into bed. You need rest. In the morning, we'll figure out a plan to help your grandparents."

Hannah yawned and opened the door. Liberty climbed out and rounded the car. With her arm around Hannah's shoulders, she led her toward the porch.

"You owe me a son." A voice startled her from behind.

Liberty whirled, peering into the darkness. Rupert's silver eyes glinted in the shadowed night. She sucked in a quick breath. Her heart pounded painfully against her ribs.

She pushed Hannah behind her and reached into the holster at the small of her back. She jerked out the Glock and aimed it at Rupert's heart.

He chuckled, his smooth, deep voice contrasting with the evil that resided in his heart. "You know you can't kill me, Liberty. You wouldn't risk that family's life, remember?"

Liberty gritted her teeth. *Bastard.* Rupert had mesmerized one of the locals—she had no idea who—to kill his family and himself if Rupert was killed. He was right, she wouldn't risk a family's life.

Damn. She lowered the gun. "Maybe not, but if you think I'm going to let you take Hannah, or me, you're out of your mind." Rupert was determined to capture Liberty, to steal her blood for his selfish purposes. He wouldn't kill her—a vampire didn't have the ability to kill a Van Helsing, except on a full moon night and only by biting her, which would kill them—but Rupert would use whatever means he could to make her suffer.

He shook his head. "I am aware it won't be easy. But when I decide to capture you, I will succeed. Right now, however, I have something else in mind." He stepped into the circle of illumination from the porch light. Evil emanated from him. "You stole Blake from me."

Hannah remained frozen and silent behind her—as if that would prevent Rupert from seizing her.

Liberty swallowed hard but stood her ground. She

spoke calmly. "Blake was a sadistic serial killer. He had to be stopped."

Pain flashed over his handsome face. "Yes. His acts could have exposed our presence. Could have ended tourism and dried up our food source. But that doesn't change the fact that he was my son, and you killed him."

She tilted her head to one side. "I'm sure the most upsetting fact is that you and Eli can no longer procreate. Now, your entire line will die out." It was a risky taunt.

Rupert laughed, and her skin crawled. "Oh, but that's where you're wrong."

Liberty snorted. "Bullshit. He was killed by a Van Helsing. His sire, and anyone he's turned, loses the ability to create vampires."

"Precisely, but I was not Blake's sire."

"What?"

"The man who turned Blake was also his biological father. My wife was an unfaithful trollop. The night her lover turned Blake, I was there. I killed him before Blake awoke. I told Blake I'd sired him. He had no reason to think otherwise."

"But… shouldn't he have known… sensed it? Isn't there some kind of special bond or something between a sire and a progeny?"

"There is, but Blake and I were close. We already shared a father/son bond. He never realized the sire bond was lacking."

Wow. She had no idea. "What about Eli? He doesn't know, does he?"

Rupert gave a cold smile. "No, he believes he's lost the ability to procreate." He curled his hand and studied his nails. "He'll be enormously pleased when I tell him the truth."

Liberty grunted a laugh. "Yes, I'm sure he'll be soooo grateful when you inform him of a truth you should have told both your sons a few hundred years ago." Realization dawned. "Is that why Blake was jealous? Because you showed Eli favoritism?"

He dropped his hand and snapped, "I didn't come here to discuss the dynamics of my relationship with my sons."

"Then what *are* you here for? What's done is done. I can't bring Blake back. And I wouldn't if I could. He was a monster." She lifted her chin and met his gaze. "So, what do you want from me?"

His mouth tightened. "I want Eli."

She shrugged. "Sorry. Eli's a grown man with a mind of his own. If you weren't such a shitty father, maybe he would still be with you."

A low growl left his throat. "I love my son. He loves me."

She snorted a laugh. "Yeah, right. If he loves you so much, then why did he leave you?"

An undetectable emotion passed through Rupert's eyes, but his voice was cool, controlled when he spoke. "You'll have to ask him. Regardless, if he returned home, to his roots, I have no doubt he would come around to my way of thinking. It's in his blood."

"And what do you think I can do about it? Even if I were willing?"

"You have a great deal of influence over Eli."

She grunted out a chuckle. "You're even crazier than I thought. Eli is egotistical and single-minded. No one has influence over him, certainly not me."

"On the contrary. He cares deeply for you. He would do anything to protect you."

Alicia Dean

Right. Granted, Eli was attracted to her, just like he was to every other female, but it went no deeper than that. "Even if that were true, how does that help you get him back?"

"It's really very simple. You come willingly with me, and I'll release you on the contingency that Eli trades himself for you. It's true, I desire you as my captive, but until I find the antidote, you aren't all that valuable to me. "

Supposedly, an antidote existed that would make Van Helsing blood safe for vampires. If that were true, and the antidote surfaced, one of Liberty's defenses against them would disappear. Not only would it be safe to drink her blood, doing so would allow vampires to see their own reflection, something they desperately desired. Even without the antidote, Rupert wanted her blood to punish errant vampires. Either way, his plan was as twisted as he was.

"Come willingly with you? Are you out of your mind?" She held up a hand. "Don't bother. I know the answer to that. And here's an answer for you, go to hell." She snatched Hannah's hand and stalked to the porch steps.

Rupert's voice stopped her. "The girl was lucky. Her grandparents will not be."

Dread chilled her blood. She whirled. "If you harm them—"

He chuckled, brows lifted in amusement. "You'll what, little hunter? Kill me? No, I don't think so." His voice hardened to steel. "Give me Eli, and her grandparents go free."

Damn if she'd let him threaten her into bending to his will. She'd save Lester and Nelda Rankin without

22

sacrificing Eli, *or* herself. She gave a satisfied smile. "What do you think Eli is going to say when I tell him about the deal you offered?"

Another growl erupted, and his eyes reddened. The flesh on his face grayed, tightening visibly. "Oh no, that wouldn't be wise."

Before Liberty could react, he zipped across the yard and snatched Hannah up by the neck. She screamed, but the sound was cut off by his hand on her throat.

"Let her go!" Liberty lunged toward him, pointing her gun at his heart. "Let her go, now!"

Without taking his eyes off Hannah, he snarled, "If you say one word about this to Eli, I'll come back and rip her head off." He released her abruptly, and she fell to the ground. She grabbed her throat and coughed, trying to catch her breath.

Liberty dropped down beside her. "Hannah? Are you all right? Can you breathe?"

She gave a small nod. Tears flowed from her eyes.

Liberty glared at Rupert. "Get the hell away from us."

"Think about my offer." He brushed his hands together. "And I'd rethink telling Eli. Not only will you jeopardize the girl, Eli will try to take matters into his own hands. And it will get him killed."

"I won't tell him." She didn't know if Rupert would kill Hannah, but she couldn't take the chance. Besides, he was right, Eli might go after him, and God knows that wouldn't end well. "But you can't force Eli to be someone, or something, he's not. He chose to leave all of that behind."

"No one can leave behind their nature. Eli's a savage."

She shook her head. "You're wrong. Eli's changed. He's not a savage."

Rupert chuckled. The sound sent chills crawling over her flesh. "You really don't know him at all."

Chapter 3

"Demons" by Imagine Dragon competed for dominance over the drunken chatter inside the nightclub. With Eli's acute hearing, even the mildest noises sounded like loud roars. But the din suited him. Sometimes, all he wanted was to be swallowed by sound and darkness.

Angelique wove through Steamy Nights between wall-to-wall bodies, her face practically glowing. He'd promised her a feeding, reward for the self-control she'd shown when Hannah and Liberty had been at the house. She'd gotten off to a rocky start, but after his warning, she'd backed off. He knew what it was like to be hungry, especially to a newbie vamp. A burning need crawled through your veins like hot lava, the smell of blood so sharp and enticing it made you salivate. He hadn't been a newbie vamp in centuries, but the hunger hadn't dissipated, he'd just learned to master it.

She'd only been a vampire for three weeks. He'd been bringing humans to her, letting her drink a little at a time, teaching her how to control the hunger. Tonight was the first time he'd taken her out of the house.

Normally, a few nights with a progeny was enough, but Angelique was a slow learner. She was impulsive, reckless. He'd had to keep her under close surveillance.

He tried to focus on Angelique, but his mind drifted to Liberty. He hoped she wouldn't do anything stupid.

He'd strangle her if she went to the compound. Actually, he wouldn't have to. She'd get herself killed.

A familiar laugh snapped his attention back to Angelique. She was pressed up against some guy on the dance floor. Her head tilted toward his neck…

Shit.

He strode onto the dance floor and grabbed her upper arm. "Come on, dance is over."

"Hey buddy." Her dance partner, a gangsta wannabe wearing a backwards cap and gold chains, puffed out his chest and balled his fists at his sides. "We weren't done. The lady can make up her own mind."

Eli ground his teeth together. "I just made it up for her. And if you want to stay healthy, you'll back the hell off."

The guy scowled. He opened his mouth, then snapped it shut. His gaze caught Eli's, and something flickered in his eyes. The boldness receded.

Eli hadn't mesmerized him, but maybe he wasn't as dumb as he looked. Perhaps gangsta-boy surmised that a confrontation wouldn't end well for him. The guy dropped his fists and stepped back.

Eli tugged Angelique over to a deserted corner and spoke quietly. "What the hell do you think you're doing? If I hadn't stopped you, you'd have eaten that guy, right there in front of everyone."

She crossed her arms and pushed out her lower lip. "You said I could feed tonight."

He shoved a hand through his hair. Christ, he hated pouting. "I also said you had to be discreet. Stick close and let me lead the way."

"But when can I eat?"

"Patience. It's all about patience, remember?"

She stomped her foot. "But I'm so hungry."

"It's part of being a vampire. You have to learn to control it."

He snagged her hand and tugged her along, scanning the room. Female laughter—amusement coated in malice—caught his attention. A few tables away sat a blonde babe. Even though she was seated, Eli could see she had a killer body, with full breasts and perfect curves. Her lips were ripe and red, her eyes the color of brilliant sapphires. She held court with four guys who panted like starving dogs.

Eli meandered nearer. The woman looked up and caught his eye. She was even more of a knock-out up close. A slow, self-satisfied smile stretched her lips. She leaned forward, letting her shimmery white blouse fall open to reveal her luscious cleavage.

Eli snorted. Such an obvious ploy. In spite of her beauty, she left him cold—colder than normal. She was too obvious, too aware of her own beauty.

"You'll have to go now," she addressed her admirers though her gaze locked on Eli.

A muscular guy at the table frowned and glanced around at his companions. "Who?"

She flicked a hand in the air as though brushing away a fly. "All of you, go."

A thin guy with a receding hairline shook his head. "But… you're *my* date."

She snickered. "If you think paying for dinner and a few drinks buys me for an entire evening, you're out of your mind. Beat it."

Red-faced, he shoved out of his chair, toppling it to the ground.

The woman laughed. "My, my, what a sore loser."

She looked at the other guys. "I said, get lost."

Among grumbles and curses, the other men scattered from the table.

"She's a total bitch," Angelique whispered. "Let me eat her."

"Hang tight." Eli strolled to the table. The blonde raised her gaze to his. "You were pretty rough on those guys."

She shrugged. "It's a woman's right to change her mind." She pushed a chair out with her foot. "Have a seat."

Eli dropped into the chair.

She leaned close and rested a hand on his forearm. "When I see something I want, I go after it."

He grinned. "And that something would…?"

"Don't play coy with me, gray eyes. You saw me looking at you. I'm Tiffany, by the way." She ran a hand up his arm and over his chest. "How about we head to your place?"

He cocked his head toward Angelique. "I'm with a… friend."

She glanced at Angelique and smiled. "Three's company."

Eli stood and held out a hand. "Never could resist a willing… participant."

Tiffany took his hand, and a slight scowl marred her forehead. People often reacted that way upon touching his cool skin. She didn't comment, didn't pull away.

He led her over to Angelique. "This is Tiffany. She's coming to my place. Care to join us?"

Angelique's smile lit up the dark club. "Sure. Let's go."

Outside, Eli helped Angelique into his corvette.

Tiffany climb into a silver Beamer. He shook his head. God, save him from materialistic bitches.

The drive was short and once home, he led the women inside.

Tiffany glanced around the living room and curled up her nose. "*This* is where you live?"

"This is it."

"It's sort of... small. And shabby." She sighed and gave a shrug. "Oh well, it's not like I'm marrying you."

God forbid. "Ah, you're accustomed to more elegant digs."

She laughed. "You could fit five houses this size in my parents' home."

"Your parents? So, it's not *you* who is rich, it's your parents."

Her lips tightened. "What's theirs is mine." A smile replaced the frown. "Especially once they're dead."

He gave a sardonic smile. "I can see how broken up you'll be when that happens."

She giggled. "You got anything to drink?"

He turned to Angelique. "Why don't you get our guest some wine."

"Be right back."

Angelique hurried into the kitchen. Eli was proud of her restraint. She hadn't jumped on the woman... yet.

Tiffany dropped onto the sofa and crossed one long leg over the other. "So, let's get the small talk out of the way. I never caught your name."

"Eli."

"Nice to meet you, Eli. You obviously aren't a local. Where are you from?"

"England."

She lifted her brows. "You're British? Where's your

accent?"

He shrugged. "After two-hundred fifty years of traveling the world, it faded."

She rolled her eyes. "Ha, funny."

Angelique stalked back into the room and held out a glass of Merlot.

Tiffany took the glass, swallowing half its contents without so much as a thank you. She frowned. "Cheap, but not bad." She glanced at Angelique, who'd moved across the room—again, showing remarkable restraint. She leaned a shoulder against the wall, hands twisting together.

"So, let's get this party started." Tiffany smiled. "She's not my usual type, a little plain for my tastes, but I'm in the mood for something… different."

Eli grunted. "Didn't your parents teach you any manners at all?"

"Why bother with manners? My daddy taught me to have sophisticated tastes. He would have fits if he knew I was slumming with an island rat."

Angelique started forward, but Eli held up a hand. "Easy."

Tiffany laughed. "Yes, down, girl." She sipped from her glass.

Eli rested his linked hands between his knees. "So, tell me, is *Daddy* here on the island with you?"

She shook her head. "No, I came on my own. Daddy and I had a little tiff, and I wanted him to worry. I chose Sang Croc because of the rumors I've heard about the Cave of Youth." Her eyes lit up. "How awesome would that be? Staying young forever?" She downed the rest of her wine and leaned toward Eli, planting a wine-soaked kiss on his mouth. She pulled back slightly and whispered, "Did we come here to talk or…?"

She kissed him again, her wet tongue darting into his mouth. Her lips smashed against his like she was grinding coffee. "Yes, baby," she murmured against his mouth. "Let's take this to the bedroom." She glanced at Angelique. "We'll let you know when we're ready for you."

Tiffany stood and gripped Eli's hand. He let her pull him to his feet.

No way in hell was he going to the bedroom with this she-devil. Time to end this. He brushed the back of his hand along her cheek, ran his gaze over her perfect features. "You really want to find the Cave of Youth?" His whisper sent her eyes dancing with greedy delight.

"You know where it is? Daddy would pay big money to find it."

Eli jerked her against his body and murmured in her ear, "Your daddy can buy you anything you want, can't he?"

"Mmmhmmm." She wrapped her arms around his neck. "Everything can be bought."

"Except immortality."

"Immorality?"

He glanced at Angelique over Tiffany's shoulder. "Time to eat."

Angelique darted across the room, pulling up directly behind Tiffany.

"What…?" Tiffany whirled around. "What did you just do?"

Angelique grinned. "Oh, it's not what I just did, it's what I'm about to do." Her face crinkled, her skin grayed, and her fangs shot out. Tiffany screamed, and Angelique sank her teeth into her neck.

Tiffany struggled uselessly against Angelique's superhuman grip. "Help! Please. Oh God…"

Eli's heart raced, and his flesh tightened as Angelique fed. He clenched his fists at his sides to keep from joining her. This was hers… all hers. This was *her* reward.

He forced himself to focus on something other than the rich, sweet smell of blood that filled the air, the exciting sound of Tiffany's cries, growing weaker…

An image of Liberty floated before him. How different tonight would have been if it were her in his arms, her lips he'd tasted.

A low growl erupted from him, and he squeezed his eyes shut. Liberty could never be his. Never would he taste her blood. Not unless he wanted to die a horrific death.

A loud sucking sound snapped his attention back.

Angelique looked at him, her breathing heavy, her red eyes narrowed. She held Tiffany's limp body. Warm dark blood coated her mouth, Tiffany's neck, her breasts.

Eli's body tensed with need, his own blood pumping through his veins with the force of a hurricane.

Angelique's expression was an odd combination of satisfied and still ravenous. "How much can I…?"

Eli clenched his jaw and gave a curt nod. "Drain her."

Chapter 4

Liberty turned her back on Rupert and assisted Hannah onto the porch. Antoine, her deceased father's Tahitian manservant, opened the door, his face drawn in concern.

He wore a robe, and though it was the middle of the night, his graying hair was neatly combed. "Miss Liberty?" He peered past them into the darkness. "What has happened?"

"Hannah was attacked. I fed her my blood, and she's recovering, but she needs rest."

Antoine wrapped an arm around Hannah and helped her inside, then eased her onto the sofa. "Rest here, young lady." He looked at Liberty. "I will prepare food."

"I'm not hungry." Hannah's voice was tiny, weak. She stared straight ahead, her expression dazed.

Liberty met Antoine's gaze. He nodded and left the room.

Liberty arranged an afghan over Hannah's thin body. "You need to eat something to get your strength up. At least try, okay?"

"I'll try."

"Good." She gave a reassuring smile. "I'll be right back."

In the kitchen, Antoine was pulling fruits and vegetables from the refrigerator.

"Need any help?" She took a seat at the bar. He

would never accept her offer. The kitchen was his domain.

"No, thank you." He looked at her over his shoulder. "But you can enlighten me as to what happened to the poor girl."

Liberty relayed what Hannah told her. "Her grandparents are still imprisoned." Her jaw clenched. "Along with who knows how many other innocent humans."

He lifted his head from the pineapple and sweet potatoes he was slicing and peered at her. After a few seconds, he said, "You have that look about you."

"What look?"

"As though you are making plans. Plans you most likely should not make."

She shrugged. "I want to help her grandparents. Eli told me some of the humans stay with the EO's willingly, but the Rankins are hostages. If I don't help them, they could die."

Frowning, he slid the food onto a plate. "Your father was aware of humans being held against their will, and while it disturbed him, he did not attempt to rescue them. He knew his calling was as a hunter. He could be of more assistance staying away from the EO's' compound. Protecting the island on nights of the full moon. You should do the same."

Liberty snorted. "You sound like Eli."

Antoine added almonds and a braised chicken breast to the plate. "I must say, I agree with Eli. Venturing to the EO's' side of the island is not safe."

Irritation flooded her. "You don't care about my well-being, all you want is for me to stay healthy so I can hunt. Just like Eli."

His lips twitched. "Yes, that is correct. Eli is only interested in your…" He gave an uncharacteristic brow wiggle, "…*hunting* skills."

Rolling her eyes, she snatched up the plate and marched the food in to Hannah. She still lay on the sofa where they'd left her, covered with the afghan. Her eyes were open, tears leaking from the corners.

Liberty settled on the edge next to her and offered the plate. "Here."

"Thanks." Hannah rose and leaned her back against the arm of the sofa and nibbled at the food. Clearly she had no enthusiasm for eating.

Liberty waited.

Hannah set her plate on the side table after finishing only a third of it.

"What happened the night you and your grandparents were attacked?" Liberty gentled her voice, but she had to ask.

Hannah sniffed. Between bouts of crying, she told Liberty about her argument with her grandparents. How she ran out of the hotel, about the encounter with the vampires. Her grandparents had come after her, and they were all kidnapped.

Hannah swiped at her eyes. "I feel terrible. If I hadn't been such a brat, this never would have happened."

Liberty patted her shoulder. "That's not true. They could have gotten you any time."

Hannah seemed unconvinced. "Eli was right. Many of the humans *want* to be there. But the rest of us…" She shuddered. "We were chained up. And, they came in after dark and… fed on us."

Liberty cringed, unable to reconcile how horrific it

must have been. "How did you escape?"

"One of the vampires took me from the basement—that's where they kept us—and took me to his room. I was terrified. I thought…" Her hands trembled, and she covered her eyes. "I thought he was going to…"

"It's okay." She took Hannah's hands in hers. "Did he?"

She shook her head. "No. There were a couple other vampires in his room, two girls and another guy. They were drinking, partying. They passed me back and forth and just kept… *feeding* off of me." Her voice rose, but she swallowed loudly and pressed on. "After a while, the others left. This vampire was set to take me back to my cell, but instead, he lay across the bed and passed out. They'd taken so much of my blood. I was weak, dizzy, but I knew that would be my only opportunity. I didn't want to leave my grandparents. I was heading to the basement to get them. But, three vampires were guarding the door. If they captured me, I wouldn't be able to save Grandma and Grandpa. I had to go, try to get help." She turned a stricken gaze to Liberty. "I shouldn't have left them." A sob tore from her throat, and tears dripped down her cheeks.

Liberty pulled her into a hug and patted her back. "Shhh… it's okay. You did the right thing. It was the only way to help them."

She nodded and pulled away. With a trembling hand, she wiped tears from her face. "Thank you. For everything."

"Of course." Liberty stood. "Come on, I'll show you to your room. Tomorrow, we'll figure out a way to rescue your grandparents."

****

Hannah slept until mid-morning. Liberty was in the kitchen drinking coffee when she came in yawning and rubbing her eyes. "I can't believe I slept so long. I didn't think I'd sleep at all with my grandparents…" She trailed off and sniffled.

"You needed it. Your body needs to heal."

Liberty rose and went to the sideboard. She glanced out the floor-to-ceiling windows. A rare thunderstorm threatened. Gray skies pressed against the opaque glass. Hopefully, the weather wouldn't hinder her plans.

She lifted the cover off a platter of ham and croissants. "Hungry?"

Hannah inhaled deeply. "Actually, this morning I am. That smells awesome."

Liberty dished ham, croissants, and fruit onto a plate and slid the food and a bottle of Noni Juice in front of Hannah.

Hannah tucked into her food, not speaking until she'd devoured every morsel. She sat back and sipped her juice.

Affection squeezed Liberty's heart. Hannah was just a child, and she'd been through so much. "Feel better?"

Her lips trembled. "I'll feel better when Grandma and Grandpa are back safe."

Liberty brushed a strand of blonde hair back from Hannah's pale face. "Don't worry, we'll save them."

"How?" She drew in a shuddering breath. "Are you going to do what Rupert said? Go along with his plan?"

Liberty winced. Last night, Hannah had apparently been aware of more than Liberty realized. "No, I'm not going to sacrifice Eli."

"Then how? If you don't, Rupert will kill them."

Liberty pushed away from the table and went to the

coffee pot to pour another cup. "Don't worry. I'll rescue your grandparents. I promise." As soon as she said the words, she wished she hadn't. Or, that she'd at least modified them. Truth was, she couldn't make any promises. She had no idea if she'd succeed in saving Lester and Nelda, or if she'd even survive. Perhaps she should have said, 'I promise I'll do my best to save them, although I'm just as likely to get them—and myself—killed.' On second thought, maybe the lie was better.

Liberty returned to the table and patted Hannah's clasped hands where they rested on the table.

Hannah lifted a blue-eyed gaze. "What about your family? You've never told me about them."

"My father is dead." Sadness at losing the man she'd known so briefly gripped her. She drew in a shuddering breath. "My mother is in Oklahoma."

"I bet you miss her. Do you guys get along?"

A lump rose to Liberty's throat. "Yes, we get along. She's my best friend. I miss her terribly."

"What do you miss most about her?"

Liberty sensed Hannah needed conversation to distract her from her fear. She thought for a moment, then smiled. "You know, it's funny, but I miss things I never dreamed I'd miss. Like, Mom always insisted that we have 'girls' night' once a week where we'd sit down to dinner together and play board games. I always thought it was lame, but…" She gave a tearful chuckle. "I'd give anything to play another stupid game of Monopoly with her."

Hannah's eyes misted over, and she squeezed Liberty's hand. "You will. And I'll see my grandparents again. We just have to believe."

****

Bianca glanced at the clock on the straw-covered wall of the tiki bar. Liberty was due in an hour. Good. She needed assistance with the mob. Someone other than that slacker, Nadia, who was all about herself and never helped out when her co-workers were slammed.

Right now, Nadia was at the bar talking to Diego. He stood with his fists clenched at his sides, his jaw tight. Big surprise. They were arguing. Bianca shook her head. Nadia was a total bitch to him. What did he see in her? Was he that enamored of her exotic beauty? The curvy body, the perfect teeth, the combination of caramel-colored skin and ocean-blue eyes was alluring, sure, but was he that shallow that her looks could keep him tied to her?

And, what was Diego doing out in the daytime? He was a vampire, for God's sake. He'd burn up in the sunlight.

She approached a table a few feet away, keeping an ear and eye focused on Diego and Nadia, only half-listening to the couple at the table as they placed their order.

"I've been waiting for you on the beach since last night and had to come in here when the sun rose." Diego's voice was tight with irritation. "And you just now show up? Now, I'm stuck here until sundown."

Nadia shrugged. "'Dat is not my pro'lem. You shoul' know I was not comin' if I din' show up by 'dis mornin'.'"

Diego let out a low growl. "It would have been nice if you'd let me know. Maybe, you know, shot me a two second text or something. You *told* me to meet you here."

"I figure since you get to be 'ere with the lovely

Bianca, you don' mind I don' show up."

Bianca's face warmed with embarrassment. Her brother, Ryan, lived with Diego, and he told her Nadia was jealous of her and Diego, but there had never been anything between them. The girl was a crack pot.

"Dammit, Nadia. I told you I'm not interested in Bianca. This petty jealousy is getting old. Bottom line, you stood me up, and now you're trying to deflect."

Nadia sighed and glanced away, like she was bored with the conversation. "You wan' me to say sorry? Dat will make it all bettah?"

Diego's handsome face had a greenish tint to it. His ebony eyes looked hollow, and dark circles rimmed them. In spite of her irritation, Bianca couldn't help but worry. He didn't look well at all. Was he ill?

Diego's voice lowered, and Bianca had to strain to hear. "You said I could feed."

"I change my min'."

"You can't keep doing this to me. I'm hungry. I agreed not to feed on another human, and I've kept that promise, yet you won't let me feed. I can't survive on animal blood alone."

Irritation surged through Bianca, and she bit her lip to keep from butting in. He seriously agreed not to feed on anyone but her? And she was withholding her blood?

"I can't talk right now." Nadia flipped her braids over her shoulder. "I 'ave work to do." She stalked away.

Diego stared after her, shaking his head.

Bianca turned in her order and headed over to Diego. "I don't know why you tolerate her rubbish."

He glanced at her, then back to where Nadia stood at a table. "I love her."

Bianca snorted a laugh. "That's not love, honey,

that's servitude."

He frowned and raked a gaze over her body. "And I guess you're such an expert on love, what with all your successful, meaningful relationships?"

A twinge pinched her heart, but she pushed it aside and lifted her chin. "You don't have to be an expert to know when someone is being a gigantic scut."

"You handle your love life, I'll handle mine."

Bianca opened her mouth to rip into him, but he looked over her shoulder, and his expression changed so drastically—from irritated to murderous—she clamped her lips shut.

She followed his gaze. His father and younger sister, Selena, had come in. The man had abused Diego his entire life until three years ago when Diego asked Eli to turn him. Recently, Diego's mother had died from heart failure. And now his sister had only him… and their asshole father, Gerardo. Diego no longer had to fear his dad, but Selena was still at his mercy. As far as Bianca knew, Gerardo had never touched her. Yet.

Diego's jaw was clenched so tightly, she worried his teeth might shatter. "I wish I could get her away from him."

"Are you afraid he'll hurt her?"

His shook his head. "Not really. I mesmerized him not to. I just hate the son of a bitch. She needs to be with someone who'll care for her, protect her. I don't trust him."

"Yes, but she loves him."

Diego snorted a laugh. "Yeah, we don't always have the best judgment when it comes to loving people."

Bianca narrowed her eyes. In spite of his earlier protests, he had to be talking about Nadia. So why the bloody hell did he stay with her? "True. But she needs the security her father brings. You can't forget what happened when your mother almost… died, and they put Selena in protective custody."

His mouth twisted. "When my mother almost *died*? Why don't you say what really happened? Mom tried to kill herself because of the way that bastard treated her."

Bianca flinched at the raw pain in his voice. "And while Selena was in that place, she—"

Diego whirled on her and grabbed her by the upper arms. His eyes were tortured. "I know, okay? You think I forgot all of that? That my little sister tried to follow in Mom's footsteps by cutting her wrists? It's not something I'll ever forget, so you don't have to remind me."

"You're hurting me," Bianca bit out between clenched lips.

Diego released her and shoved a hand through his hair. He squeezed his eyes shut, then opened them. Pain simmered in their dark depths. "I'm sorry. I didn't mean to. I just… don't like to think about that time. About what might have happened." He grunted and shook his head. "I don't understand why she'd want so badly to go back to a piece of shit like him."

Bianca placed a hand on his forearm. His skin felt clammy. She stuffed back her irritation at Nadia for withholding her blood, and at him for allowing her to control him. "I know. I'm sorry. But he's her father. You became a vampire and left home. She lost one parent. She probably feels… abandoned. He's her security."

Diego let out a long breath. "I guess so. But if he ever hurts her…"

"I know. We just have to hope he doesn't." She

42

released his arm. "I'd better go take their order."

Bianca forced a smile when she approached the Ortegas' table. "Hey guys, how are you? Can I get you something to drink?"

Selena was a pretty girl with dark hair and eyes like Diego's, carrying a few extra pounds on her short frame. She was thirteen and blossoming into a lovely young woman. She didn't speak, or raise her head.

Bianca frowned. "Everything okay?"

Gerardo answered for her, his gaze on his daughter's bowed head. "Everything is good."

Bianca tossed him an irritated glance. "I was talking to Selena."

His eyes squinted, and he clenched the edge of the table like he was holding back from punching her. He was thin and wiry, with black hair shot through with gray. His features were similar to Diego's, but harsher with age and meanness. He was a tough guy when it came to beating women and children, but he wouldn't dare challenge his vampire son. Knowing Diego was nearby gave Bianca the courage to stand up to him. That, and the fact she couldn't abide abusive cowards.

She looked back at Selena. "Are you all right? Because, you can tell me if you're not."

She nodded and lifted her head, offering Bianca a small, unconvincing smile. "I'm fine." Selena reached for the menu, and the sleeve of her blouse pulled back. A dark purple bruise marred her forearm. Selena quickly shoved her sleeve back down. Her gaze flew to her dad, then to Bianca.

Bianca's breath caught in her throat. Had the son of a bitch hurt her? Bianca glanced over her shoulder. Diego still stood by the bar, glaring at his father. If he saw the bruise, he wouldn't ask questions, he would pounce. "Hey, Selena, want to come to the ladies' room with me? We've got this great new set of lotions I want to show you."

Before the girl could respond, Gerardo said, "She's fine right here."

Bianca ignored him and extended a hand. "Come on, you'll love them."

Selena looked to her father, to Bianca, then back to her father. Drawing in an audible breath, she took Bianca's hand and let her lead her to the ladies' room.

The door shut behind them. The room was empty, but might not be for long. Bianca took Selena's sleeve and shoved it back. More bruises ran from her elbow to her shoulder.

Selena tugged away and covered them with her sleeve. She raised tear-filled eyes to Bianca. "Please don't tell Diego. He'll kill Dad."

The anger surging through Bianca made it difficult to keep from killing him herself. "I thought Diego mesmerized him not to hurt you."

She wiped tears from her eyes. "He did. But, somehow it didn't work. Dad was really drunk when Diego did it. Maybe that kept him from focusing enough for it to take?" She drew in a trembling breath. "Anyway, Dad never used to hit me but, well, I've been hanging out with my friends and staying out later than I'm supposed to. The other night, Dad came looking for me. I was at the beach with some older guys." Her face flushed pink. "He was over the top furious. When he got me home…" New tears surfaced. "I—I shouldn't have talked back to him. I guess he just lost his temper. He said he was sorry."

"Oh pig's arse if he's sorry. Diego needs to know."

"No, please. Diego will kill him!"

"No less than he deserves."

"He was drinking. He didn't mean it. He won't do it again. He promised. Never again."

"He won't stop. He's a chicken shit mongrel. I have to tell Diego."

"Please, please don't." She grabbed Bianca's arm and dug her fingernails into her flesh. "I'm begging you. It was a onetime thing. He was really sorry. Please promise me you won't tell anyone. If you do, I… I'll kill myself."

"Selena! Don't say that."

"I swear, I will." Tears flowed from her eyes. Her lips trembled, and her voice dropped to a whisper. "If Diego killed my dad, I… I wouldn't want to live. And I swear to God I'll do it. Promise me you won't!"

Bianca's gaze dropped to the razor scars still visible on Selena's wrists. Would she really try to off herself again? No, surely she wouldn't. But if she did, and Bianca was the cause…

Bianca eased loose from Selena's grip and huffed out a frustrated sigh. "Okay, for now, I won't tell. But, I want you to promise me, if it ever happens again, you let me know. If you don't, and I find out…"

"I promise."

"I'm going to see you every day. Check on you."

"You don't need to. I'll be fine."

"You either agree, or I tell him right now."

"All right. You can. But we can't let Dad know you're keeping an eye on me."

"Right, then. We'd better get back out there." Bianca slid a tube of mango scented lotion from her apron pocket. "Here, put some of this on in case he asks. Don't want him to chuck a wobbly."

For the first time, Selena smiled a real smile. "The way you talk cracks me up." She held her hand out, and Bianca dabbed a spot of lotion in her palm. Selena rubbed her hands together while Bianca held the door open for her.

Diego was waiting outside the ladies' room. His gaze went from Bianca to his sister. He gave Selena a tight hug, then set her away from him. "Hey, squirt. How's it going?"

"Great."

"You sure?" He frowned up at Bianca. "What were you two talking about?"

Selena shrugged. "Not much. Bianca was just telling me about this guy she's seeing."

His face darkened like a thunder cloud. "Really, Bianca? She's thirteen years old. A little young to hear the details of your... escapades."

Bianca tightened her fists at her side. He must think she was the biggest whore in town. "Yeah, well, you know how us slutty girls are. We like everybody to know."

He cut his eyes to his sister. "Sorry, just forget whatever she told you. You don't want to be like that."

What was his problem? They used to be mates. When had he turned into a complete douche? She sniffed back tears. "Right. You don't want to be like me."

"She's awesome, Diego." Selena took Bianca's hand and squeezed. "You're a jerk. You hurt her feelings."

He searched Bianca's face as if to ferret out the truth. Bianca forced nonchalance into her expression.

She'd sooner die than let him know she gave a fig what he thought.

Apparently satisfied, he said, "Nah. She doesn't care what I say."

"You're just a great big ass, you know it?" Selena shook her head. "I gotta go. Dad's waiting."

She stomped off to the table, and Diego lifted his hands in the air and let them drop to his sides. "Look, if I hurt your feelings…"

"I don't give a stuff what you say. Gotta get to work." She didn't spare him a second glance as she stalked away.

Chapter 5

Liberty dressed in her uniform of a short black skirt and button-up blouse covered in pink and white orchids, then climbed into her car and headed to The Perfect Getaway. She hated leaving Hannah, but she was in good hands with Antoine. Not only was Liberty scheduled to work, she needed to speak with Ryan.

The sun was a blaze of oranges, blues, and purples, as it slowly sank into the horizon. Torch lights flamed around the straw façade of the bar. Inside, customers filled the bamboo tables, and a line of them waited in the small sitting area, some sipping on colorful umbrella drinks. The dinner rush had started early.

Ryan's sister and Liberty's best friend on the island, Bianca, caught Liberty's eye when she came in. "So glad you're here, love. This place is going bonkers. Strap your apron on and give me a hand, would you?"

"Sure." Liberty grabbed an apron and tied it around her waist.

Ryan was behind the bar, wearing a short-sleeved tropical shirt. He winked and gave her a grin. She loved his smile, the way his dark eyes crinkled at the corners. They weren't a couple, but she liked him. A lot. She just wasn't sure how much, or that she was ready for a relationship.

A steady stream of customers prevented her from the opportunity to speak with Ryan. She'd have to wait until after work. They'd have more time then anyway.

When business slowed enough for a break, she stepped outside for fresh air. The back of the tiki bar faced a line of palm trees nestled in white sand that glittered in the moonlight. The island was so beautiful. Liberty still couldn't believe she actually lived in such a paradise.

The back door opened, and Nadia slipped outside. The gorgeous Jamaican had taken an instant dislike to her. Liberty tensed like she did every time she was around her.

Nadia flung her dark braids over her shoulder and pulled a joint out of her apron pocket.

She lit it, took a drag, and held it in. She offered the joint. Liberty shook her head. "No, thanks."

"Huh." Nadia squinted through the smoke and spoke while holding her breath. "You dit not take it just to be my friend. You 'ave mind of your own. I like dat you do."

"What makes you think I even want to be your friend?"

Nadia exhaled, and her white teeth flashed in the darkness. "You want to be everybody friend cheah leadah."

Liberty smiled. "You're not entirely wrong."

"I am never wrong." She took another hit off the joint. "I 'erd about how you save dat girl. How you wan' to save her family."

"Yes."

"Very brave of you. EO's are dangerous."

"So am I." Liberty was surprised to find she actually meant it. She had a long way to go, but she'd come a long way too. Vampires had as much reason to fear her as she did them. "No matter what, I can't let those people die."

Nadia chuckled, tapped the fire from the joint, and slid it back in her pocket. "No, but maybe *you* die."

Which would probably be Nadia's preference. "Maybe."

Nadia shrugged. "And maybe not. Who knows, right? Break over, cheah leadah. Back to work."

Liberty took a deep, cleansing breath of the night air, then followed Nadia inside.

A few hours later, the restaurant cleared out, giving Liberty her opportunity to speak with Ryan. She approached as he was wiping down the bar.

"Hey, how's it going?" A hint of pain hovered in his brown eyes. She wished she could take it away, but giving false hope was just as cruel. Besides, he'd hurt her too. She wasn't ready to give him another chance. "Crazy night, huh?"

"Yeah. Crazy." She shook her money-stuffed apron. "But, cha'ching, right?"

He laughed. "That's what it's all about." He threw the towel over his shoulder and leaned his hands on the bar, revealing the Australian flag tattoo on his muscled forearm. "What did you need to talk to me about?"

She jerked her gaze away from the sexy tattoo and slid onto a barstool. "I need you to tell me where Rupert's compound is."

He narrowed his eyes. "Eli knows where it is. Did you ask him?"

"I can't ask him. I don't want him to know I'm looking for it."

"You're not planning on doing something stupid, are you?"

"It's not stupid."

"If you're planning to try to rescue the Rankins, then yes, it's stupid. Eli will be mad as a cut snake when he finds out."

She blew a breath out between pursed lips. "I have to help them. All I need you to do is tell me where I can find them."

"Are you nuts?"

"Do you think I can stand by and let those poor people be slaughtered?"

"You can't save everyone, Liberty."

She let out a sigh and tucked a hank of hair behind her ear. "Of course not, but I've looked into Hannah's face. If it were my family, I'd want someone to save them."

"You can't do this on your own. You need to let Eli help."

"No way. He'll just try to stop me. He doesn't give a damn about her grandparents. Tell me where the compound is."

Ryan rubbed his hands over his face and shook his head. "On one condition."

"And that is?" She had a feeling she wouldn't like his answer.

"I go with you."

"No, no way. I won't let you take that kind of risk."

His jaw tightened. "I get it. You're the big bad hunter, and I'm just a bloody deadhead."

"Well, I don't know what that is." She spoke lightly. "But I'm pretty sure you aren't one." She laid her hand over his. "Please. I just can't risk anyone else."

He pulled his hand away and crossed his arms over his chest. "Sorry. That's the deal. Take it or leave it."

"Ugh… okay, fine. You can go." She glanced

around the bar, spotting Bianca stocking condiments on one of the tables. "But your sister will kill me if anything happens to you."

"You don't have to worry about that." He grinned. "We'll probably both die. If the EO's don't kill us." He leaned forward and whispered in her ear. "Eli will."

She popped him on the arm with her fist. "Great, way to build my confidence." She slid off the stool "We'll go in the morning since the vampires don't do sun."

"Tomorrow? You're not wasting any time."

"I don't have any time to waste. Those savages are treating her grandparents like a smorgasbord." She drew in a trembling breath. "How long can they survive something like that?"

****

The alarm's buzz punctured the quiet, but Liberty was already awake. She'd been too keyed up and hardly slept all night.

She climbed out of bed and took a quick shower. After dressing in boots, jeans, and black T-shirt, she slid her Glock in the holster at her waist, grabbed her rucksack, then quietly tiptoed downstairs. She couldn't risk encountering Antoine. He didn't approve of her plan any more than Eli did. She stopped by the kitchen for granola bars, fruit, and water.

Ryan was waiting at the end of the drive like she'd requested. His hair was damp. He wore jeans and a snug charcoal gray T-shirt. A gray backpack hung over his shoulder.

"You ready?" He placed a quick kiss on her cheek, and she inhaled the scent of bergamot and sandalwood from his soap. Delighted quivers danced over her flesh.

"I think so. You parked down the road, right?"

He gave her a dimpled smile, his dark eyes crinkling at the corners. "Of course, your wish is my command, milady."

Her pulse raced, and she took a deep, steadying breath, then nodded. "Great. Let's do this."

They had to walk. No roads led to that side of the island. She wasn't looking forward to a trek through the forest, but it was the only route.

Ryan peered closely at her. "It's a long jaunt. Are you sure you're up for this?"

"I'm sure." She had to be. Nelda's and Lester's lives depended on it.

At the back of the property, she ducked into the shed and slipped a knife into the sheath at her waist and one in each boot, grabbed her bow, and filled her quiver with arrows. She exited the shed and followed Ryan into the forest behind the house. Almost immediately, the sun was obliterated as though night had fallen. A light rain fell, and the faint rumble of thunder rolled above, but the canopy of trees kept them mostly dry.

They'd walked for a few hours, barely speaking, keeping at a speedy pace. Brambles from the pretty, but thorny, purple bougainvillea snagged her clothing. Liberty's legs burned, and her lungs felt like they'd burst. But she wouldn't complain, wouldn't stop.

"You okay?"

Ryan's gentle voice spoke from beside her.

"I'm…" She took a breath and swallowed humid air. "I'm fine."

He took her arm. "You look exhausted. Let's have a break."

She wiped sweat from her brow with the back of her

hand. "We have to get there before sundown." *Before the Rankins were killed*. If they weren't already. What if they were too late?

Ryan touched her arm, stopping her. "You might be right as rain, but I'm knackered." He drew in a labored breath. "I need just a moment to regroup. Neither of us will be any good if we arrive half-dead."

"Fine. Just a few minutes." The burning ache in her legs grew more noticeable once she stopped moving. She dropped her pack and sank to the ground, leaning against it. Big mistake. She wanted nothing more than to curl up on the damp, soft grass and snooze.

Ryan settled beside her. He retrieved a bottle of Noni juice and a granola bar from his pack. "Here you go, love. To get your strength up."

She took them from him, and their fingers brushed. In spite of her exhaustion, a tremor of electricity skipped over her flesh. "Thank you." She met his eyes, then quickly looked away.

He took a long gulp of his juice. "So, what's the plan, boss?"

She sipped her drink and took a bite out of the granola bar. She had no idea what they'd be facing when they arrived. All she knew was, at least until the sun went down, it wouldn't be vampires. "I'm not exactly sure."

"We're about an hour out still." Ryan peered up at the glimmer of sky peeking through the thick treetops. "We've got time before dark, but we'll have to find them quickly. And without raising attention of the humans on guard."

"I don't get it. Why would humans align with someone as evil as Rupert?"

His white teeth flashed in a smile. "You don't think

only vampires are despicable assholes, do you?"

She grimaced. "No, I suppose not. Humans have been doing evil since the beginning of time."

"And Rupert pays them well. He needs minions who can perform the tasks vampires can't, or at least who can be outside in the sunlight when vampires can't."

Of course, a twisted, brilliant mind like Rupert's would consider all possibilities. They finished eating. Liberty drained the remainder of the bottle and reluctantly rose to her feet. "I guess we should get moving."

They set out once more, and, in less than an hour, came upon a clearing. In the distance, stood a gigantic iron gate. Blooming shrubs and leafy trees lined the fence.

"This is it?" Liberty halted, her voice a whisper.

"Yes, that's Rupert's compound," Ryan whispered back.

A structure that could only be described as a castle stood thirty yards from the entrance to the gate. Several smaller huts were nestled side by side on either end of the grounds. The late afternoon sun glinted off silver spires that surrounded the home. Liberty counted half a dozen armed men patrolling at various areas along the fence.

"Impossible." Her heart sank into her stomach. No way could they get around these men and inside the gates.

"I didn't come this far with you to see you give up." Ryan took her hand and tugged her behind a tree. He cupped her head in his palms and stared into her eyes. "We're here. You're Liberty Van Helsing, Vampire Hunter. We'll not be defeated."

His dark eyes held confidence and faith. Two things she desperately craved at the moment. If he believed that strongly in her, she wouldn't let him down.

"Okay. Let's do this." She pulled away and peered around the grounds. "Hannah told me they were kept in the basement. And that the access is at the rear of the house."

"The fence stretches around the entire property. It will take too long to circle around back, and I'm not sure we'd be able to get through the fence anyhow. I say we go through the gate and make a straight beeline."

Liberty chewed her lower lip, squinting at the guards. "And, in order to do so, we'll have to take these guys out."

"That's right." Ryan held up his Ruger. "Three for each of us." He winked. "They don't stand a chance."

She forced a smile, wishing she shared his confidence.

"I'll take the three on the south end." She withdrew two arrows from the quiver, nocking one and leaving the other to dangle from her release hand. "Meet me at the rear of the hut on the far right." Once they got to the gate, *if* they were successful in taking out the guards, they still had to find the basement without being seen. Who knew what other sentries were posted closer to the house? What had she gotten herself into? She swallowed her groan.

Keeping low, she duck-walked toward the fence where a guy wearing a ball cap, dark brown shirt, and jeans held a rifle across his chest. His two buddies were stationed several feet away. She slipped up to a section of fence hidden behind a small copse of trees. She climbed over and dropped down on the other side close behind him. He whirled, mouth open set to shout, lifting his gun at the same time.

Liberty released the arrow, automatically nocking the second one.

Yes. The arrow found its mark, dead center of his chest. He let out a small grunt and dropped to the ground.

Liberty slipped behind a tree, searching out the other two. Damn. They stood right next to one another. How the hell could she take two of them out at once?

She clenched her jaw. She could do this. She'd taken out vampires. Of course she could handle a couple of humans.

But, she'd had the cover of darkness on her side. And she hadn't been as apprehensive. Was it because taking out humans was a completely different prospect? After all, they were true, living *people*…

No matter. These assholes worked for Rupert. They had harmed, maybe killed, innocent people. Gritting her teeth, she stepped from behind the bush and aimed. The man facing her lifted his gun, but she released the arrow and caught him in the center of the forehead before he had a chance to pull the trigger. His partner whipped around, gun cocked.

She ducked back behind the tree.

His voice carried to her. "Come on, be a good girl and show yourself so I don't have to come in after you." What an idiot. Did he really think she would obey his command? "Just put your hands up and step out, nice and easy."

Her gun would draw the attention of others. She couldn't take that chance. But she had to move fast. She'd wasted enough time already, and she might not fare well against more guards. Besides she couldn't do anything that would put Ryan in jeopardy. He was good with a bow, and a knife, but he wasn't as experienced as she was. What if he was hurt… what if he needed her?

No, she had to get this done. Quickly and quietly. She whipped the blade from her boot and held it shoulder high. The stench of sweat and fear from the guard wafted over as he drew closer. His breathing pinpointed his location. *Come on, only a couple more feet.* She lunged from behind the trunk, launching the knife at his chest in the same motion. Another strike. He let out a pained shout, firing off a shot before crumpling to the dirt.

"Shit!" She peered around. Had the gunshot drawn attention? They were several yards from the other houses. Nothing stirred. Thankfully, the noise seemed to have gone unnoticed.

Now, to find Ryan.

She averted her eyes from the blood spilling out of the man's chest and swallowed back nausea. No time for weakness.

On stealthy, quick steps, she hurried to the hut. Ryan waited, one hand gripping his bicep. Blood dripped from beneath his fingers.

"Ryan! You're hurt." She gingerly took his arm.

"I'm fine." He tried to jerk away.

She closed her eyes to steady the dizziness threatening her equilibrium. The coppery scent of blood assaulted her. Revulsion shuddered along her spine. With a surge of determination, she took control. "You're not fine. Hold on." She dug into her pack and pulled out a vial of blood. "Drink this."

He pushed her hand aside. "You need to save that for someone in true danger. This is just a scratch."

But the pain in his eyes and the tightness of his jaw

said he was lying. "Let me at least wrap it for you." She used her knife to cut a strip off the bottom of her T-shirt and quickly bound his arm, drawing slow, deep breaths through her nose to keep from passing out.

When she finished, Ryan tucked a finger beneath her chin and tilted her head up. "You okay?"

She tightened her lips. "Fine, you?"

"I'm good. Let's go."

They used the cover of the foliage to traverse the grounds until they were behind the house. They'd walked half the length of the mansion before Liberty spotted a door set into the ground. She reached out and stopped Ryan with a hand on his arm, then pointed. He nodded, and they each drew their guns.

Chapter 6

Ryan tugged on the door while Liberty scanned the area for guards. A movement from the right made her whirl, gun pointed. A man stalked toward them, holding a gun out in front. "Hey! What do you—"

Not wanting to make a sound and draw attention, Liberty pulled her knife from its scabbard and threw it, sticking his chest before he could react. He landed with a thud. She replaced the knife with one from her boot.

Ryan looked over his shoulder, but didn't speak. He tugged open the basement door.

Darkness greeted them, along with the scent of unwashed bodies and rusty blood.

With shallow breaths, she followed Ryan into the belly of darkness.

Shuffling sounds came to her, but she couldn't see anything for several moments. Then, her eyes adjusted to the dimness. She counted some twenty people, ranging in age eighteen or so to sixty-ish, lining the dank, stone walls. Some were holding onto one another. Shackles on their feet and hands were connected to the walls.

"Don't be afraid," Liberty said softly. "We're here to get you out." Hannah had mentioned the chains, but actually seeing it... humans treated worse than animals...

Liberty gritted her teeth. If Rupert were here right now, she'd gut him. How could anyone—

Oh God. Eli had once been just like Rupert. He'd kept humans captive. Feeding from them. Discarding them like trash. Nausea choked her, and she swallowed bile. *Eli had changed.* He wasn't that way anymore.

But the thought that he had been…

She shook her head. No time to dwell on that now.

Since Hannah had mentioned the chains, Ryan brought bolt cutters. The Rankins were in a corner, slumped on the ground, arms gripping one another.

Nelda rose unsteadily to her feet, metal scraping concrete, and squinted at Liberty. "Liberty? It is you. What are you doing here? Where's Hannah? Is she okay?"

"She's fine. I'll explain everything later. We need to get you out of here." She surveyed the other captives. "All of you."

They set to work, and several minutes later, the chains fell away, freeing the captives.

Releasing the hostages was the easy part. They still had to navigate to the other side of the island without running into trouble. They would be well away before dark. Anyone who challenged them would be human. She and Ryan should be able to handle them. She hoped.

Sympathy squeezed her chest as they led the weak, frail humans from the basement. The hostages squinted at the sun and blinked rapidly, as if they hadn't seen sunlight in a while.

"Come on," she said softly. "Let's move."

She and Ryan herded them away from the mansion. Rather than chancing retracing their path to the front gate, they went the shorter route toward the woods at the back of the property and made it to the fence without encountering any other guards. Once there, Ryan cut away enough of the bars that everyone could squeeze through, one at a time. Liberty kept an eye out behind them, stomach clenched at the thought of discovery. An eternity passed before the last person stepped through the fence.

She had a chance to study the hostages once they were safely into the trees. They seemed in decent health. The others were younger than the Rankins. No doubt the elderly couple had been targeted by Rupert simply due to Hannah's connection to Liberty. The bastard.

Among the group was a young woman, probably a few years older than Liberty. Beneath the grime and tangled blonde hair, the girl was pretty... gorgeous, Liberty reluctantly acknowledged. Obviously, Ryan noticed as well. He'd remained glued to her side since they'd left the compound. A few times, Liberty looked back to see him grab the girl's arm and help her over a tangle of tree roots. A split second of jealousy seized her, but she pushed it aside. Ryan was not hers. It was none of her business if he was attracted to another girl, even if it did annoy the hell out of her.

"...I can't thank you enough."

Liberty snapped her attention back to Nelda. She'd totally zoned out on their conversation after she explained the events leading up to their rescue. She hoped the woman hadn't asked her a direct question. After the ordeal the poor thing had been through, the last thing Liberty wanted was to make her feel she didn't care.

She smiled. "Glad to help."

"Hannah's so brave, but she took a big chance. Thank you for taking care of my little girl. And for rescuing us."

"It's okay, really." The woman's praise made her uncomfortable. "Please. You don't have to thank me."

They pushed as far as they could before they had to take a rest. The hostages couldn't keep up the pace she and Ryan had. They were too weak, some were clearly out of shape.

She and Ryan passed out the drinks and food they'd brought. They didn't have enough for everyone, so the group had to share. She wished they'd brought more, but they didn't know how many people they'd be bringing back, and they could only carry so much. At least the hostages would have a little sustenance until they could get back to town and receive proper care.

Cracking branches startled her, and she glanced back through the trees. Four men headed in their direction.

"Ryan." Liberty urgently motioned toward the intruders.

Quickly, they shepherded everyone behind trees, then hid and waited.

A bullet whizzed by, hitting the tree above her head. She squelched a cry and fired at one of the men. He went down, and she aimed again. Before she could squeeze the trigger, someone grabbed her from behind and clamped a hand over her mouth, the other arm across her breasts.

She struggled against his hold and bit down on his fingers. He cursed and jerked his hand from her mouth, but she couldn't get free. Ryan spotted them and aimed.

He couldn't take the shot without hitting her. He started toward them, but a bearded wide-shouldered man jumped him. Ryan tumbled to the ground, and the assailant leapt on top of him.

"Ryan!" Liberty struggled harder and elbowed her

captor in the side. He grunted, and she stomped her foot in his instep. With a yelp, he loosed his hold. She spun and kicked him in the chest. He stumbled back, then lunged and knocked her down, landing on top of her. He was three times her size. His weight squeezed the breath from her. He punched her in the face, and her head snapped to the side. Pain exploded in her jaw. She squeezed her eyes shut to hold back tears. He drew his arm back for another blow.

Her mind went back to Eli's lesson. *Feel the blood coursing through your veins...* Van Helsing blood. She focused on the warmth surging through her body, the power of her heredity. Her muscles tingled and tightened. His fist flew toward her face, and she let out a ferocious growl and grabbed his hand, stopping its forward momentum. His eyes rounded in surprise. She shoved him, and he flew backward, landing on the ground with a thud. Before he could react, she jumped to her feet and jerked her knife from its sheath.

He rose and came toward her. She drove the knife into his chest. Blood leaked around the handle onto her hand. He thumped to the ground and Liberty shuddered. She wiped her hand off on his shirt and whirled. Ryan was still struggling with his attacker. He was pinned beneath the man, his hand scrambling for the gun lying just out of reach.

Heart in her throat, she yanked out her Glock, but Ryan reached his own weapon, aimed, then fired. The man flew back, a hole in his neck pumping blood.

Legs wobbling, Liberty collapsed to the ground and fought to draw in a breath.

Ryan knelt beside her. "Are you hit?"

She shook her head. "I'm fine. Just... winded."

A frown marred his expression as he gently touched her jaw. She winced.

His mouth tightened. "You're hurt. The son of a bitch."

She squeezed his hand. "It's just a scratch."

He gave a brief nod, but worry shone in his dark eyes. "You up for the trek home before we have any more uninvited guests?"

She pushed to her feet. "Yeah, ready." Shaky, sore and exhausted, excitement still coursed through her. She'd found her Van Helsing strength, just like Eli promised. She didn't share it with Ryan. She wanted Eli to be the first to know.

****

Just before they reached town, Liberty called Antoine and asked him to bring Hannah to the hospital. They decided everyone should to be seen by doctors, especially Lester, who'd grown weaker by the hour. By the time they arrived at the hospital, he was barely able to walk. His skin was pale and clammy, his breathing irregular. Ryan half-led, half carried him through the emergency room doors.

Hannah waited just inside. She ran to them. "Oh my God, I was so worried about you." She went into her grandmother's arms, sobbing against her bosom, then pulled back and looked at her grandfather. "Grandpa? What's wrong?"

Liberty stepped forward. "We need to get him checked—"

With a groan, Lester collapsed. Hannah screamed.

Doctor Lemanu burst through the swinging doors next to the check-in desk, followed by two nurses pushing a gurney. Ryan helped the doctor lift Lester onto the stretcher, and the nurses wheeled him through the double doors. Before the doors closed behind him, Dr. Lemanu said to Nelda, "We will take good care of him. Wait here and I will come back and speak with you soon."

Hannah led her grandmother to the waiting room chairs. The other hostages checked in at the ER desk, and Liberty lowered wearily into a seat between Antoine and Ryan. Her jaw ached like a mother. No telling how it looked. It felt swollen to twice its size.

Antoine put his hand over hers. "You should go home and rest."

She shook her head. "I want to wait and find out about Lester."

"It could be a while. You are about to keel over. And your face… What happ—" He grimaced. "Never mind. I do not want to know. Go home. Rest. I will stay here with Hannah, and we will update you."

Liberty let out a sigh. "We don't even have a car here."

Antoine reached into his pocket and handed Ryan a set of keys. "Take mine. It is a few rows back in the ER parking lot. You can come back and get us after you have had a nap."

A nap… mmm… sounded like heaven.

She kissed Antoine on the cheek. "Thank you."

His face flushed. He cleared his throat and gave a quick nod.

Ryan stood, slipped an arm around her waist, and led her outside. Smoky, dark clouds like bits of lace drifted across the half moon. She drew in a deep breath of the fresh air, feeling marginally better just being out of the hospital… and the jungle.

They reached the car, and Ryan was unlocking the door, when a flash of movement from the corner of her eye made her jump.

Eli appeared before her. "What the hell is going on? Where have you been?" His fierce silver gaze swung from her to Ryan, then back.

Ryan's mouth opened, but before he could speak, Eli flung up a hand, palm out. "No. You don't have to tell me. I know where you've been, and you're an idiot."

Ryan's face flushed, and his mouth compressed. "Look, I just didn't want—"

Eli dove at Ryan. He jerked him up by the shirt collar and dangled him above the ground.

"Eli!" Liberty rushed over and grabbed Eli's arm. It felt like cold stone beneath her fingertips. "Stop it! Leave him alone. It was my idea. He only went along to keep me from going by myself."

Eli glared at her. "Yeah, I'm aware of that. Help with something *you* shouldn't have been doing in the first place." He shook Ryan and growled, "What the hell were you thinking, you stupid son of a bitch?" He threw him off like a discarded toy.

Ryan stumbled, then came to his feet, red-faced. "No one got hurt, so you just need to chill."

Eli latched onto Liberty's arm, none too gently. He narrowed his eyes on her jaw. "No one got hurt, huh?"

Liberty yanked her arm from him. "It's not a big deal."

"The hell it isn't." He punched Ryan in the face. Ryan flew back, landing hard on the concrete.

Liberty gasped. "Ryan!"

Ryan rose and wiped the blood from his mouth. He glared at Eli.

Blood pumping with rage, Liberty whirled on Eli. "You're being ridiculous! I chose to go. For God's sake, Eli, I'm a hunter. An actual hunt is more dangerous than what I did today."

His fists tightened, and she thought he would go after Ryan again. But he turned his fury on her. "Yes, but you have to hunt. This was a foolhardy mission that wasn't necessary."

The weariness caught up. Her shoulders fell. "We saved the lives of twenty people. You call that unnecessary?"

He sighed and scraped a hand over his eyes. "If something happens to you, where will the natives be?"

"Yeah, right." Ryan's derisive laughter cut through the night. He stalked up to Eli and shoved his shoulders.

Eli stumbled back, and Liberty held her breath. Was Ryan *insane*?

"You're full of shit," Ryan bit out. "Why don't you stop pretending you're only interested in her as a hunter?"

Eli glared at Ryan, then tossed Liberty a look and shook his head. Without another word, he took off, disappearing into the night.

Liberty peered at Ryan's bloodied, swollen lip. She gently touched her fingers to it. "Are you okay?"

He shoved her hand away. "I'm fine. I'm not that fragile." He let out a frustrated huff. "It's been a long day. Let's get you home and call it a night." He stormed around the car and climbed inside, slamming the door.

Liberty gritted her teeth and slid into the passenger seat. Sometimes, she wanted to throttle them both.

She hadn't had a chance to tell Eli about tapping into her strength. *Good.* The way he'd behaved tonight, she didn't want to talk to him about anything.

Chapter 7

Eli tried to tamp down his fury. What the hell. It was her own damned hide. He was tired of trying to protect it. She couldn't keep doing such foolish things. Taking away the EO's food source? Rupert would be enraged. Maybe Eli could calm him before he did something... lethal.

He headed to his father's, even though he'd prefer to have his fingernails ripped out with plyers.

Rupert opened the door, his eyes widening in surprise. "Well, well, well. To what do I owe this unexpected visit?"

"We need to talk."

He stepped back. "It's been a while since you journeyed to this side of the island. Dare I hope you've come to rejoin us?" He smiled. "Or, might this have something to do with the theft of my humans?"

Eli let the phrase 'my humans' roll around his mind. There was a time, not so long ago, that he'd thought of them the same way. Now, it made him uncomfortable... angry. "They aren't *your* humans. You kidnapped them, held them against their will."

Rupert chuckled and waved a hand in the air. "Semantics. Would you like a drink?"

"I won't be long."

"I've never known you to turn down fifty-year-old scotch. Surely you have time for one?" He poured a couple of fingers and handed it to Eli. "You know, you're starting to sound like a human. You do realize, they're nothing more than a source of sustenance."

Eli's mouth twisted. "Come on, even you don't believe that. It makes you feel better to think of them that way."

"There's no other way to think of them."

"Not even Danielle Van Helsing?"

A slight narrowing of his eyes and tightening of his jaw were the only indications of how the name affected him. "I don't know what you mean."

"Bullshit. You were in love with her. She was the only human who ever meant anything to you, and Victor won her heart. You've never gotten over it."

"That's ridiculous," Rupert insisted, but his gaze fell away with the lie.

"Is it?" Eli sipped his drink. He had the old man cornered. "That's also why you've got a fondness for Liberty. Because she's Danielle's daughter."

Rupert harrumphed. "Unlike you, I would never be fond of a hunter." He spat the word like it was vile.

"Let this go. Gather new humans and don't retaliate."

"You know I can't do that."

"You could."

Rupert refilled his glass. "That's not like me at all. What do I get in return?"

"You get your only son, not hating you."

Again, Rupert chuckled. "Hmmm. I'm afraid that ship has sailed." He advanced on Eli, and Eli had to force himself to maintain his position. He wouldn't let the old man back him up. "Liberty is not only a hunter, but she killed your brother. Thanks to her, Blake's entire line will die out."

"Blake was a murdering—" Eli stopped. "Blake's line? What about our line?"

"Ah. About that… good news, my boy." Rupert clapped a hand on Eli's shoulder. Eli jerked away. "Our line is intact."

"What are you talking about?"

"I'm not the one who turned Blake."

"Then who did?"

"Blake didn't belong to me. Your mother was a whore. His biological father turned him."

Eli's gut clenched, and he tightened his fist around the glass but didn't respond to the insult to his mother. The son of a bitch wasn't worth it. He let the news sink in. On one hand, he was relieved he could still turn humans. On the other, his mother had cheated on his father… But then, who could blame her. Rupert had been as big an asshole as a human as he was as a vampire.

"Blake never said—"

Rupert shook his head. "He died believing I was his real father. And that I'd turned him. I came upon the fiend who'd stolen what was rightfully mine. He'd bitten Blake, and was waiting for him to waken. I killed him. When Blake woke up, he had no memory of the bastard feeding on him. I told him I'd sired him."

Just like Rupert, to take what he wanted without a second thought. "Since you aren't his sire, then his line dying out doesn't affect you all that much."

"It doesn't change the fact that she killed him… the boy I raised as my own."

Eli didn't bother reminding him a second time that Blake murdered innocents, leaving their bodies for all to see… or that he'd framed Eli for the murders. Rupert chose to see things as he wanted, regardless of the truth. "I'm asking you, as your son, to let this go."

Rupert's brows lifted. "As my son? You haven't played the "son card" in a while."

Eli resisted an impulse to wipe the smirk from Rupert's face. Swallowing the urge to vomit, he said, "Please."

"I'll consider it—on one condition. You come back."

Eli snorted a laugh. "You're out of your mind. I will *never* come back. Not after what you did."

"Ah, you must be referring to the unfortunate incident with the lovely Christelle?"

"Incident? You murdered the woman I loved."

Rupert shrugged. "I tried to teach you not to play with your food."

White hot rage blinded Eli. He roared and flew into Rupert, knocking him to the floor. Rupert's glass went airborne as Eli pounded his fists into the hated features. He'd only gotten in a few punches when the door banged back. Hands grabbed his arms and yanked him off his father. Four guards held him.

Rupert climbed to his feet. He brushed his hands over his suit jacket and smoothed back his hair. His eyes shot fury, but outwardly, he remained cool and calm.

Eli jerked against the guards' iron grip, but they were vampires, and he was no match for the four of them. He panted, glaring at his father. "I'll never come back, you son of a bitch. And I'll watch over Liberty. You'll never get near her."

Rupert's only response was a smug grin.

The guards yanked Eli through the door. Rupert's shout followed him down the hallway, "Remember son, women aren't worth it. They aren't to be trusted. You'll learn soon enough."

****

Liberty's body ached all over. She'd thought herself in better shape, but walking thirty miles and being attacked by half a dozen assholes was more than she could handle. The desire to stay in bed and recuperate was tempting, but her shift at the tiki bar started soon.

Groaning, she climbed from bed. After a quick shower, she gulped down three cups of coffee and headed out.

Ryan was behind the bar, a white bandage around his bicep. She only had a moment before she'd have customers in her section, but she wanted to make sure he was okay. She approached the bar. He winked. Her stomach fluttered, and she drew in a breath to steady it.

"How are you feeling?" he asked before she could ask him.

"I'm fine. How about you?"

He shrugged, then winced. "A touch sore, but I'll make it."

"How's Jenna?" She tried to keep her tone casual, tried not to let on that there was a part of her that hoped he would say he had no idea, that he hadn't seen her since they left the hospital and didn't intend to.

She must have convinced herself that was exactly what he'd say, because his words took her by surprise.

"She's coming along okay. A little dehydrated. They released her from the hospital, and she had nowhere to stay, so she's crashing at our place."

Our place? She was *living* with him? "Oh? What's her story? Does she live on the island?"

"No. She was vacationing here when she was

kidnapped. Her family thought she'd died." A smile lit his face. "You can imagine their joy when they learned she was alive."

"Yeah, I can imagine."

"Anyhow, they'll collect her in a few days. In the meantime, she has no money, no place to live."

"Well, other than with you."

"Right. Other than with me."

Liberty blanked her expression. Inside, she was seething, even though she had no right to be. Jenna was a beautiful girl, and Ryan was... well, he was sexy as hell. With the two of them sharing quarters for days... She was no fortunate teller, but she was pretty sure she could predict what would happen between them.

"That's, uh... great. Awesome that she has you." Did her voice sound as phony to him as it did to her?

He narrowed his eyes. "You okay?"

"Sure, yeah." She glanced over her shoulder. "I'd better get to work. Looks like I have a table."

"Talk to you later."

"Yeah, later."

In moments, the place was packed. Liberty was too busy to be pissed that Ryan had potentially found someone. She had no right to be pissed, even if she did have time. After all, she'd let him go. So why did it *feel* like she had a right to be pissed?

The rush was just winding down, and she delivered the check to her last table. They didn't close for another few hours, and she would no doubt have more customers, but for now, she had a reprieve. She trudged to the bar and leaned her elbows on the top. She just needed thirty seconds to breathe...

"Liberty."

The voice came from over her shoulder. A familiar, female voice. Her knees trembled, and she whipped around. "Mom?"

She looked beautiful. Her silky blonde hair was longer, and the style suited her. Dressed in jeans and a red button-up shirt, she appeared much younger than her forty-one years. She held out her arms, and Liberty rushed into them. Her mother held her tightly. Liberty hugged her back, crying into her neck, not caring that everyone in the place was staring.

Liberty drew back and wiped tears from her cheeks. "I can't believe this. What are you doing here?"

Danielle cupped Liberty's cheek in her soft, warm hand. "You didn't think I was going to miss my baby girl's birthday did you?"

"Oh, my gosh! I had no idea you were coming. You should've let me know. I would've taken off work." Happiness bloomed, and she thought she'd float off the ground.

"Honey, it's fine. I'll be here a few weeks, so we'll have plenty of time together. I wanted to surprise you."

"Well, you definitely surprised me. I'm so happy you're here." Now that the elation of seeing her mother after so long had worn off, worry took its place. It was true, Liberty was happy she was here. But the island was a dangerous place, especially for anyone Liberty cared about. How would she keep her mother safe for two weeks?

"I'm happy I'm here too."

"Did you come alone?"

Pink colored her cheeks. "Not exactly." She glanced behind her and motioned with her hand.

A man with reddish brown hair and goatee, wearing

a tropical, sea-shell adorned shirt, joined them.

Danielle took his hand. "Sweetie, I'd, um, like you to meet Neal Murray. Neal, my daughter, Liberty."

Judging by the blush on her mother's face, this guy was more than just a traveling companion. All through Liberty's childhood, she'd never even known of Danielle to date. And now, the minute Liberty was gone, she hooked up with some dufus? Liberty smiled to cover her disconcertion. She should be happy for her mother. Besides, she had no way of knowing if he was a dufus. He could be a really awesome guy. Liberty stuck her hand out. "Nice to meet you."

"Forget that. Family doesn't shake hands." Before she knew what was happening, he'd brought her into a bear hug and squeezed her so hard she lost her breath.

Okay, definitely a dufus.

He pulled back and studied her, keeping ahold of her hands. "I've heard so much about you, Liberty, I feel like I know you."

Well she didn't know him, and he wasn't family. She tugged her hands loose and glanced at Danielle. Why would her mother bring some guy when Liberty hadn't seen her in months? Didn't she deserve that time with *just* her mother?

A frown appeared between her mother's brows. "Everything okay, sweetie?"

Liberty forced aside her pissiness. Making her mom feel bad was not the best way to start their visit. Liberty was too happy she was here to let him bother her. She smiled. "I'm so glad you were able to come with Mom so we can get to know one another better."

"Me too!" He slipped an arm around Danielle, and she blushed again. "I'm crazy about this girl here, and I want you to like me."

"I'm sure I will." *Not*.

Her mother's amber eyes sparkled. "Neal is a reporter. When I told him I wanted to visit you, he researched the island. Did you know that there is a cave here that is supposedly filled with some kind of anti-aging water? It's ridiculous, I know, but he just couldn't resist the idea of doing a story on this legendary Cave of Youth."

The smile froze on Liberty's face, and her skin went cold. The last thing they needed was a nosy reporter digging around. It was bad enough that her mom had brought a boyfriend. But a *reporter* boyfriend?

Liberty gave a casual shrug. "It's just a legend, a ploy to bring visitors to the island."

Neal let out a belly laugh. "Well, of course it's not real, but I still want to see it. It'll make a hell'uva story, and I can write off my trip. Have you been there? Maybe you could show me the way. I'd like to take my camera guy out there."

Camera guy? Just freakin' great. "No, like I said, it's only a rumor."

"Well, as many people as you're bound to know on the island, surely someone can help us find it."

Liberty had heard mention of the cave, but had never been there and didn't know where it was. And, she didn't intend to ask. She didn't know how she was going to get out of it, but she was *not* going to escort this loser to the Cave of Youth and let him make a big splash on TV.

She turned to her mother, ignoring him. "Where's your luggage? I get off soon, and I can take you to the house."

"Oh, we're not staying with you, sweetheart. We

wouldn't want to impose."

"You wouldn't be imposing. The house is huge. I want to spend time with you. I would love it if you stayed with me."

A shadow passed over her mother's face. "We already have hotel reservations. Besides, it wouldn't seem right staying in your… uh… father's house."

When Liberty received a cryptic note from her unknown father, her mother had sworn that her father had died and that whoever this man was, he was an imposter. Upset with her mother, believing she'd withheld the truth, Liberty had traveled to the island. She'd discovered the existence of vampires, and learned that her mother had been mesmerized to forget they ever lived on the island. Sadly, she'd barely started getting to know Victor Van Helsing before he died. Danielle didn't believe Victor was her father, but had apparently decided to humor her.

Although… something in her expression… She seemed uncertain… uncomfortable. Like, maybe… while she didn't want to believe, somewhere deep down, she really did?

"Mom… will you please stay with me?" Liberty sounded petulant, but she couldn't help it. "I've missed you so much, and I want to spend all the time I can with you." Maybe Jerome would give her a few days off… Yeah, fat chance.

Danielle bit her lip, looked back at Neal, then nodded. "Sure, honey. We'll stay with you. I want to spend as much time as possible with you too."

"Awesome! I'll ask my boss if I can leave early. We're slow right now, and I don't have any tables. I could show you guys the island."

"Great." Neal beamed. "We can ask around and find out the location of the Cave of Youth."

Liberty held back an eye-roll. "Sure yeah, we can ask." But she'd make damn sure they didn't find it.

Chapter 8

Jerome refused to let Liberty off early, but her mother and Neal waited at the Getaway until she finished her shift. After her last customers left, she found them at the bar talking with Ryan.

"I just have to finish up my side work and we can get out of here."

"You go on," Ryan said. "I'll take care of your side work."

"Oh no, I couldn't ask you to do that."

"You didn't ask. I'm offering. Now, go, before I change my mind."

Her mother's brows rose, and a knowing look came into her eyes. "Well, that's very nice of you, Ryan."

He shrugged. "Don't be fooled by my selfless gesture. She'll owe me big time." He winked.

"I'm sure I will." Liberty smiled. "Okay then, thanks, Ryan." She turned to her mom. "You ready?"

"I need to visit the ladies room first." She looked pointedly at Liberty. "Maybe you could show me where it is?"

"Of course."

Inside the restroom, Danielle leaned her bottom against the counter and crossed her arms. "So, tell me. What's the deal with you and Ryan? He's adorable."

"Yes, he's most definitely adorable. We dated, but nothing serious."

"And you let a guy like that go? With those looks, that accent, and he's nice on top of it?"

Liberty blew out a breath between pursed lips. "Ryan's great. But actually, he dumped me. Then, he wanted me back, but I couldn't trust him." Telling her mom he dumped her because he was mesmerized by a vampire wouldn't do. Nor could she admit that she was attracted to said vampire, who was anything *but* nice.

"Everyone makes mistakes, you know. He seems like a genuinely good guy. And trust me, those don't come along every day."

"I realize that." She was afraid to discuss her love life with her mother, afraid she'd be tempted to confess her confusing feelings about Eli. "Hey, we can talk about that later, right? Let's get out of here. I'm starving. I know this great seafood place that makes an awesome Mahana Cocktail."

"Cocktail? You're too young to drink."

Liberty grinned. "Not on Sang Croc I'm not."

Her mom's eyes narrowed. "I don't know if I'm happy about that."

Liberty hooked her arm through her mother's. "You don't have to be. I'll be happy for both of us."

Danielle's tension loosened, and she chuckled. "I suppose you're mature enough to handle a few drinks." They walked to the door together, but Danielle hesitated before opening it. "Listen, I don't know what the deal is with this man you think was your father. But, it's obvious in the brief time you knew him you cared for him. I can tell you're happy here. So if it makes you feel better to believe he was your father then we will leave it at that."

"Works for me." Since she couldn't explain the truth, Liberty had to be content with that concession.

The restaurant was crowded, and it took an hour before they were seated, but the food was totally worth the wait. The pineapple/vanilla Mahanas were a hit. Liberty limited herself to two; she didn't want to get tipsy in front of her mother. After stuffing herself on roasted Mahi Mahi with passion fruit, sautéed spinach and moist, delicious coconut bread, Liberty agreed to splitting a slice of Key Lime pie with Neal. For that brief moment, with the tart, delectable, creamy perfection resting on her tongue, she forgot she despised her mother's new guy.

By the time the dessert disappeared, she was reminded.

Danielle covered Neal's hand and smiled at Liberty, her dark amber eyes sparkling. "Neal has a surprise for you, and you'll be so excited!"

How could a guy she didn't even know have a surprise that would excite her? She forced a polite smile. "Oh? A surprise?"

A beaming grin stretched across his face. "That's right. Sunday night, I'm going to give you the biggest birthday party you've ever seen." He spread his arms wide, his expression filled with anticipation.

"Uh... Sunday night?" Her heart dropped to her stomach. Sunday was the full moon. She couldn't attend a party... she'd be hunting vampires. "I'm afraid Sunday night won't really work. The islanders have a tradition where they, and tourists, stay in. Most of the businesses shut down."

He worked a toothpick around in his mouth and his expression migrated from excited, to crestfallen, to sardonic in the span of ten seconds. "Stay inside? That's the dumbest thing I've ever heard."

"It's not dumb. It's based on some kind of long ago lore about a monster who stalked the island on full moon nights. The inhabitants have honored the tradition for centuries. Out of respect, those who visit still honor it." That was partially true. The tradition was based on lore, but the main reason they still honored it was because they didn't want people devoured by ravenous vampires, but she couldn't explain that to Dufus.

"Oh, well…" His voice dripped sarcasm. "When you put it like that, it's not dumb at all." He gave a scoffing laugh. "Come on, you have to admit, that's kind of silly. It's your birthday, and you shouldn't let some stupid tradition spoil it for you."

Liberty slowly counted to ten. "To the natives, it's not stupid. And, now that I live here, I feel I should respect the islanders and their beliefs. So if it's all the same to you, I prefer not having my birthday party on Sunday night. We can do it the night before. Or after." She rushed on when he opened his mouth. "Besides, since they *do* have the tradition, I doubt anyone would come."

A hard look came into his eyes. "It's all been set, and we're not changing it. A birthday isn't special if it's not on *the* night. Just tell the locals it's my fault. I'm sure they'll understand." He tossed a few bills into the ticket book and leaned back, draping an arm over the back of her mother's chair. "And as far as people not showing up, I'm somewhat of a celebrity. I'm sure they'll break tradition to attend a party I'm throwing."

Arrogant ass. Liberty lifted her brows and turned to her mother. Her face was flushed, and she shifted in her seat, but didn't meet Liberty's eyes. Was she really going along with this guy? What was he trying to prove?

Liberty smiled sweetly. "Thank you, but no, I prefer not to have a party that night."

Neal glared at her mother and Danielle drew in a deep breath. She looked from Liberty, to Neal, then back. "Honey, don't be rude. Neal went through a lot of trouble to… to make this happen… for me. Trust me, you're going to love it." The look on her mother's face was so hopeful, Liberty hated to spoil it. But no way in hell was she letting anyone give her a party on the full moon night. It was *not* going to happen.

"Well, I appreciate the gesture but I feel pretty strongly about honoring their tradition."

Danielle shot her a crestfallen look.

Liberty ignored it and plowed on. "If you choose to go ahead and throw my party that night. I'm afraid I won't be there."

Neal took a deep breath and let it out slowly. "This is my first time on the island and I am throwing a party, whether or not it's a birthday party for you. I was trying to do something nice for you, but if you choose to stay home, that's your prerogative."

Tears glimmered in her mother's eyes. She sniffed. "Please, both of you. Can't we work this out?"

Liberty nearly groaned. She was stuck. If she chose not to attend, things would be even worse. The EO's would have free reign to devour every human at the party. Damn him.

She sighed. "I'm sorry, you're right. That was rude of me. I appreciate the offer, and I would love to celebrate my birthday on Sunday night. Thank you." She clasped her hands together in her lap to keep from slapping the self-satisfied smirk off his face.

****

Once her mother and Neal were asleep, Liberty called Eli.

He answered with, "I'm still pissed at you."

She rolled her eyes. "Well, get over it. We have a situation."

"You *had* a situation. And you handled it very badly."

She huffed out a frustrated sigh. "This is worse. My mother arrived on the island last night. She brought some asshole who's supposed to be her boyfriend. He's a reporter. He has a camera guy coming next week. They want to do a story on the Cave of Youth."

He grunted. "Well, that sucks."

"That's not the worst of it. He's determined to throw a birthday party for me."

"And you called to invite me?"

"I called so you could help me stop it."

"Why? I thought you were all giddy about the big day."

"He's throwing it *on* my birthday. The night of the full moon."

"Son of a bitch."

"Exactly."

"Didn't you tell him he couldn't?"

"Of course I did. But he's kind of a dick. Seems to be accustomed to getting his way."

"Okay, I'm on it."

"On it? What are you going to do?"

"Take him out."

"Take him out? You mean… kill him?"

"Well, I don't mean to dinner and a movie. That's why you called, right?"

She growled inwardly. Good Lord… "No! I don't

want you to kill him."

"Then what do you want?"

"I want you to mesmerize him, him and my mom, to forget about the party, change his mind, whatever you need to do."

"You're no fun at all."

"Whatever. So, you'll do it, right?"

"Now?"

"They're in bed right now."

"Well, I can't go out once the sun comes up. Want me to come spend the night so I'll be there in the morning?"

His low, husky words send a shiver over her spine. She cleared her throat. "No, I don't think that will be necessary."

"So what's your plan?"

"I can either invite them to your house, or you can come over in the morning before the sun comes up."

"Number one, how are you going to get them to my place? Number two, I'll have to stay at your house until sundown."

"So what do you suggest?"

Her bedroom door opened. She spun and slapped a hand to her chest.

Eli stood in the doorway, holding the phone to his ear, grinning like he'd scored a winning touchdown. "Since I'm here, I might as well stay the night."

She dropped the phone from her ear and tossed it on the bed. "Dammit, Eli! I said no."

"This makes more sense. You want a favor from me, then you'll do it my way."

"You'll still have to stay here all day once the sun comes up."

Alicia Dean

"I'll mesmerize them and be gone before the sun comes up."

"I see you've thought of everything."

"I always do."

Her nerves jumped. Eli was in her *bedroom*. "Uh, okay. You can sleep down the hall in one of the guest rooms."

"I don't sleep at night."

"Fine. You can *hang out* in the guest room down the hall."

"What's wrong?" He strolled over and slipped a hand beneath her hair, cupping the back of her head. "Don't trust yourself if I stay in your room?"

Her breath caught. She dropped her gaze and pulled away. "Knock it off." She moved to the door. "Get out before someone finds you in here."

"What if they find me in the hallway?"

"I guess you'll have to hurry so they don't."

"I could do that or…"

"Or what?"

He closed his eyes, breathed deeply, and held out his arms. His body wavered, and a creaking sound filled the room. She shuddered. She knew what was coming.

He morphed into a bat and hovered for a moment in the air. She could swear he grinned. Then he flew from the room.

She clenched her fists until her nails dug into her palms. Sometimes, she wanted to strangle him.

****

The next morning, Liberty went into her mom's room. "Hey, Mom. Wake up."

Danielle groaned and burrowed more deeply into the covers.

Liberty shook her shoulder. "A friend came by for breakfast. Come on, I want you to meet him, but he only has a little while before he has to leave."

Her mother blinked sleepily. "Honey, we're on vacation. Seriously? Five a.m.?"

"Please. I really want you and Neal to meet him."

She sat up and yawned, then rubbed her hands over her face. "Okay. Neal is an early riser anyway, he'll be pleased." She climbed from bed. "I should get dressed. I can't meet him like this. I'll just be a minute."

Liberty waited while Danielle brushed her teeth and dressed in jeans and a sweatshirt, then ran a brush through her hair. They left the room and met Neal in the hallway. He smiled. "Well, how'd she get you out of bed so early?"

Danielle yawned. "Good question."

He chuckled and slid an arm around her. "Aw, come on. We'll get some coffee in you and you'll be fine."

Downstairs, Eli sat at the table while Antoine worked his magic at the stove, whipping up something that smelled delicious.

Liberty held out a hand. "Mom, Neal, meet Eli Barkley. Eli, meet my mother Danielle Delacort and her… friend, Neal Murray."

Eli's smile would have seemed genuine if she hadn't known him so well. He appeared friendly… cordial. *Nice*. "Pleased to meet you. I'm the mayor's son… uh, well, stepson. Hence the different last names." His smile grew wider.

Danielle lifted her brows, much the way she had when she'd met Ryan. She now seemed wide awake. "Mayor's stepson, huh?" She blinked at Liberty. "Goodness, you've certainly met some wonderful friends since you've been here."

Eli took Liberty's hand and put it to his chest. "Oh, I'd like to think your daughter and I are more than just friends."

Danielle's eyes widened. "Oh, is that right?"

Liberty frowned and snatched her hand away. "We're *just* friends. Eli thinks he's funny."

He winked at her mom and she actually *blushed*.

They took seats at the table, and Neal lifted a ceramic carafe. "Who wants coffee?" He filled their cups while Antoine set fluffy eggs, bacon, and smoked breadfruit on the table.

Neal shoveled in a mouthful of eggs, then pointed his fork at Eli. "What do you do for a living?"

Eli spread his arms wide. "I don't have to make a living. I get by on my charm and good looks."

Liberty sputtered and choked on a drink of coffee. "*Right…*"

Eli cocked a grin and said to Neal, "I hear you're giving our girl here a birthday party Sunday night."

"Yes, it's going to be a blowout." He withdrew a pink sheet of paper from the pocket of his robe. "Check this out."

"What's that?" Liberty narrowed her eyes on the paper.

"Fliers about your party. We paid a couple of natives to post them all over Sang Croc."

Liberty's breath caught. She snagged Eli's gaze.

His lips tightened. "You—what? When are they going to post them?"

"They started last night. Not sure if they finished. If not, they'll finish them up this morning." He smiled and chucked Liberty on the chin. "Don't worry, girlie, there'll be a ton of people there."

"*Great*." He acted as though she hadn't totally opposed the party, like he hadn't forced it on her. Ugh…

Her mother squeezed his hand. "Isn't he wonderful?"

Liberty forced a fake smile. "The *best*."

Eli lifted his coffee in a toast. "Well, *girlie*, looks like your birthday bash is on."

Liberty gritted her teeth. "Yes, it does."

"Unless… we go to plan A?" He grinned.

"Absolutely not."

Danielle glanced from one to the other. "What are you two talking about?"

"It's nothing. Just an inside joke." He turned to Liberty. "It's preferable than the alternative. Come on, you barely know the guy."

"What guy?" Neal said. "What's going on?"

Eli closed his eyes and shook his head, letting out a heavy sigh. "I said, don't worry about it." He stared into Neal's eyes. "You'll remain silent. And sit there without saying anything, and—"

Liberty shot a glance at her mom. What the hell was he doing? "Eli, you can't—"

He lifted a hand, palm up, still holding Neal's gaze. "Bup, bup, let me handle this. Or I swear, Plan A is on."

Liberty clamped her mouth shut and crossed her arms over her chest.

Eli continued. "You'll forget everything you're about to see and hear."

Neal nodded. "I'll forget everything."

Danielle frowned. "Liberty, what's going—"

Eli faced her mother. "Look at me, Danielle." She did. "You'll also be quiet and forget everything you're about to see and hear."

Her mom nodded as well and fell silent.

Eli grinned. "Now, we can talk without interruption."

Liberty grunted. "You couldn't have just excused yourself?"

"Nah, not as much fun." He glanced at the window where the pre-dawn duskiness lingered. "As John Wayne said, we're burning daylight. I need to get out of here soon, so we have to figure this out. If we don't get him to cancel the party, I swear, I'll kill him. His life isn't as important as all the victims who will be turned and all the people who will die just because he wants to have a party."

She huffed out a breath. "There has to be another way."

"Then think quickly."

"Why can't you just mesmerize him to change his mind about the party and revise the fliers? He can still have the party but on a different night."

Eli paused. "Damn, that could work."

"You don't sound happy."

He shrugged. "You know how much I like drama." He said to Neal, "You listening?"

Neal nodded.

"You'll reschedule Liberty's party to—" He glanced at Liberty.

"Friday night," she said.

He turned back to Neal. "Friday. Two nights before the full moon. Tell those islanders who hung the fliers to change the date on them. Understand?" Neal nodded again. "Everything Liberty and I have discussed is forgotten."

"Forgotten."

"Good." Eli gave a satisfied nod. "Oh, and every time you hear "All about that Bass," you'll break out in the chicken dance."

"Eli!" Liberty gasped.

"Come on, I should get *something* for my efforts here. You never want me to have any fun."

Liberty rolled her eyes.

To her mother, he repeated what he'd said to Neal. Thankfully, minus the chicken dance part.

Neal and Danielle blinked, and the dazed expressions left their faces.

"I have an idea," Neal said. "Why don't we have the party on Friday instead of Sunday? I know Sunday is your actual birthday, but Fridays are better for parties, don't you think?"

Danielle clapped her hands together. "I think that's a fantastic idea."

A mischievous glint came into Eli's eyes. "I don't know. It isn't quite as special if it's not on her actual—"

What the…? Liberty kicked him under the table.

He grunted and clenched his teeth. "Although, you have a point. Friday sounds great." He winked, then stood. "Thanks for breakfast, but I gotta run."

Liberty rose. "Give my love to the mayor."

"Will do." A devilish grin appeared. "Oh yeah, he said to give you a kiss for him."

Her heart sped up, and her eyes rounded. Eli leaned close, his gaze locking on hers. Her lips tingled, damn them. His ascent took an eternity. Lips hovering a smidgen from hers, he paused and changed course, leaving a friendly, chaste kiss on her cheek. She tamped down disappointment and fought to control her breathing, trying to pretend the *almost* kiss hadn't affected her, but judging by the gleam in Eli's eyes, he knew.

Chapter 9

Later that night, Eli called her. "Put on something pretty and come over."

"What? Why?"

"You'll see."

"But, Mom is here. I need to spend time with her."

"She and Douche are going out. I overheard them talking this morning. No more excuses. Hurry up."

She bit her lip. She didn't really want to make excuses. She wanted to go see Eli. Even if she didn't *want* to want to.

She slipped on a silky green dress and t-strap shoes, then drove to Eli's. She remembered on the way that she still hadn't told him about tapping into her strength. If he could keep from pissing her off for five minutes, she'd tell him tonight.

At his door, she smoothed down the skirt of her dress, more nervous than she should be. Being around Eli did funny things to her insides. She didn't know what to call them, but couldn't deny they were there.

He opened the door, wearing faded jeans and a black shirt, with the first few buttons undone and the sleeves rolled up. Her eyes were drawn to the sun tattoo on his muscled forearm. Why would he have a tattoo of something he longed for, but could never experience? Masochistic much?

He stood staring at her. For so long, she shifted in

discomfort. "Hi, uh, can I come in?"

"Oh, yeah, sure." He stepped back. "Sorry. You look… incredible."

Warmth stole up her neck. "Well, you said to wear something pretty."

"I did." His eyes raked her body. "And you did."

She crossed the threshold and looked around. "Where is Angelique?"

"With a babysitter."

Liberty chuckled. "Why do you have to watch over her? You always have to do that when you turn someone?"

"No. A few days are usually enough, but Angelique is a bit of a problem child." A slight curl tipped his lips.

Obviously, he was fond of his progeny. Hopefully, in nothing more than a brotherly way.

An amazing fragrance drifted to her. "Are you cooking dinner?"

"I am. You didn't know I had a hidden talent, did you?"

She dropped her purse on a side table. "No, I didn't. What are you making? Smells delicious."

"Lobster tails and fafa."

Fafa was an island specialty prepared with spinach and pork. Antoine had made it for her, but she never would have pictured Eli cooking it… well, cooking *anything*.

"Sounds great. What's the occasion?"

"I wanted to make you a birthday dinner. I'm sure it's been stressful hiding so many things from your mother. I figured you needed an evening to relax and be yourself."

She quirked an eyebrow. "I thought you didn't care

that it was my birthday."

He shrugged. "I don't. But I care that you care."

She pursed her lips and considered his words, then nodded. "I guess I'll take that." She handed him a bottle of wine. "I brought this."

He glanced at the label. "White wine."

"Well, you know how I am about the red."

"Yeah, yeah, too much like the color of blood, which makes it all the more appetizing to me." He grinned. "Have a seat and I'll pour." At the bar, he opened the bottle, filled two glasses, and handed her one.

She thanked him and settled onto the sofa. "I forgot to tell you, when Ryan and I rescued—"

He shot her a dark look.

"Sorry. What's done is done, and I didn't die. Anyway, some guards came after us, and we fought them, just the two of us. I was able to tap into my powers. Not as much as I would have liked, but I did it."

A genuine smile lit his face, his gray eyes glinting like forged steel. "I knew you could do it. And you'll continue to improve." He lifted his glass. "To you."

They clinked glasses, and she sipped. The wine was delicious, warming her insides. Contentment rolled through her.

Eli set his goblet on an end table next to the sofa. "I have something for you." He opened a small drawer in the table and retrieved a package wrapped in colorful metallic birthday paper. A hopeful expression came over his features, and for the first time since she'd met him, he looked… boyish.

"Eli… I didn't expect…" She took the package, flustered and touched. For someone who had been so callous about her birthday, he was going all out.

"It's no big deal. Open it."

Her fingers shook as she gingerly removed the paper, revealing a small jewelry box. Her heart fluttered. Jewelry from a guy. That meant… something. Although she wasn't sure what, exactly.

She opened the box and gasped. A silver necklace held a charm cutout in the shape of the state of Oklahoma, with a tiny silver heart dangling in the center. She looked up at him, awe keeping her silent.

A slight tint of pink touched his face. "I know you're homesick. I thought this might… I don't know… help a little."

Tears stung the backs of her eyes. She blinked them away. "Thank you. It's… beautiful. So thoughtful of you." Impulsively, she leaned forward and kissed his cheek. Tempted to let her lips linger against his strong jaw, she quickly pulled back.

He cleared his throat and gave a nod. "You're welcome." He stood. "I'd better go check on dinner." He disappeared into the kitchen.

While he was gone, she slipped the necklace on. The cold silver warmed against her flesh. She fingered the charm and smiled. *He cares… I know he does…*

He re-entered the living room, and she abruptly released the pendant, wiping the smile from her face.

He settled back onto the sofa. "Dinner will be ready in a few minutes."

"Great. I'm starving." She considered telling him about Rupert's visit, but between the wine and her relaxed state, she was afraid she might slip and reveal everything. What would he do if he knew his father had asked her to turn herself over to entice Eli back? Whatever he did, it wouldn't be pretty… or safe. Eli harbored a lot of anger against Rupert. He'd been wounded deeply by his father, badly enough to make him switch sides. Whatever had occurred, it must have been disastrous.

She sipped more wine. "What happened between you and your father? What made you defect from his… cult?"

He chuckled. "Not exactly a cult. But close enough, I guess." He drained the glass then held it up, frowning. "Sorry, I've tried to be polite, but this isn't really my thing. Mind if I switch to scotch?"

She gestured with her hand. "Be my guest. Mr. Avoidance."

He moved to a liquor cabinet, pulled out a tumbler and the scotch and poured a generous amount. "Mr. Avoidance?"

"Yeah. You didn't answer my question. What happened between you and your father?"

He stared into his glass, not speaking for several moments. "It doesn't matter."

She set her wine on the table and went to stand beside him. Placing her hand on the side of his face, she lifted his head. "Yes, it does. It was obviously something big. Something that mattered a great deal. You'll feel better if you tell me."

He stepped away. "Dinner should be ready."

She shook her head and stalked over and snatched up her purse. "You know, suddenly I'm not hungry anymore."

"Hey, what's wrong?"

She whirled to face him. "I thought we were friends. I mean, yeah, we have our disagreements from time to time, but I thought we'd gotten pretty close. Yet you won't open up to me. Ever." She swallowed back disappointment. "I guess you don't trust me."

He placed a hand on her arm. "Come on. I trust you."

She wiped her eyes. "Right."

"I do. It's just…" He drew in a deep breath and slowly let it out. "I don't talk about that. To anyone."

She rested a hand on his chest and met his gaze. His heartbeat quickened beneath her palm. "I'm not just anyone."

His lips tightened in a reluctant grin. "No, no you're not."

"So will you trust me? Tell me?"

"I'll make a deal. How about if we enjoy a nice dinner and afterward, I'll tell you."

Although inordinately pleased, she kept her voice level. "Sounds great." Finally, she was chipping away at the hard veneer he'd erected.

Dinner was better than she expected. Eli was a surprisingly fabulous chef. Succulent lobster tails and fafa were accompanied by soft, crusty baguettes. Shortly after she arrived on the island, she'd learned that the boxes outside homes that looked like mail boxes, were actually bread boxes where fresh French baguettes were delivered twice a day—a treat she had to enjoy sparingly to avoid packing on extra pounds.

When they finished, Eli took her plate to the sink. "I have a chocolate mousse for dessert. You in?"

Speaking of extra pounds… But, she was weak when it came to chocolate… or pretty much any food, for that matter. Good thing she worked out. She sighed in defeat and grinned. "When am I *not* in for chocolate?"

His returning grin made her heart skip. He brought two crystal dessert glasses and set one in front of each of them.

The chocolate mousse was divine. She closed her eyes and all but moaned when she swallowed the last bite. "You are an amazing cook."

"Thanks. I can't disagree."

She laughed. "And modest."

He pushed back from the table and held out a hand. "Shall we retire to the living room?"

"Sure." She placed her hand in his. "Where you'll tell me what happened between you and Rupert?"

The humor left his expression, and he gave a reluctant nod. "Yeah. I'll tell you."

In the living room, he punched buttons on an MP3 player, then stood staring down into the fireplace. "Bloodstream" by Ed Sheeran played, and she wondered... was he thinking of the bad blood between him and his father?

Finally, he came over and lowered next to her on the sofa. After taking a deep breath, he began speaking. "A few years ago, I fell in love... with a human. Her name was Christelle."

Christelle. She'd bet the girl was as gorgeous as the name. A sliver of jealousy pricked her. Some woman had penetrated his hard surface, and he'd fallen in love. Liberty shoved aside the voice that asked, *why can't it be me?* Attempting to keep her voice neutral, she said, "I'm sure she was beautiful."

"She was. It wasn't just that, though. She was smart. Fun to be around. She made me feel... almost human."

She lifted her brows. "You wanted to feel human?"

He chuckled. "I never thought I did. But when I was with her? Yeah, maybe a little." He sat forward, linked his fingers, and leaned his elbows on his knees. "Rupert

101

hated her. He hated all humans, but especially her. He couldn't stand the thought of me with a human."

Silence fell between them. She waited.

"One night I was to meet her in the forest. We had a special place we'd go to be alone. Without other vampires, other humans. Just the two of us."

"I heard before I even reached the clearing. Her. Screaming." He screwed his eyes tightly shut and let out a breath. "I rushed to the sound. She was lying in a pool of blood. Her throat had nearly been ripped out."

Liberty gasped. "She… died?"

His jaw clenched. "I thought she was dead. She was barely holding on. I heard footsteps and turned around. I launched into the man coming toward us." His gaze rested on Liberty. "It was your father."

"My… my father?" Surely he hadn't… *No!* Christelle was attacked by a vampire. No way would her father have hurt an innocent girl.

Eli nodded. "I was so blind with rage, so distraught, I couldn't think. Couldn't focus. I had my hands around his neck. Choking him. Lightly at first, I wanted him to suffer for a long time. Finally, through the haze, I made out his words."

He pushed to his feet and paced across the floor. "He was trying to tell me he could save her." Eli scraped his hands through his hair. "Reality set in. I knew he hadn't hurt her. It had to be a vampire. I released him. He knelt beside her and fed her his blood. And… she recovered. I was so relieved, so grateful. This man who had been my sworn enemy had saved the woman I loved."

"So, she was okay? Where is she now?"

He stopped in front of the sofa and stared down at her. The look in his eyes was intense… tortured. "She told me who attacked her. It was Rupert."

Liberty squeezed her eyes shut. Somehow, she had guessed that was what he'd say. "And that's why you left?"

"Not right away. I took her home, made her lock the doors. Promised I'd be back soon. Then, I confronted him. I flaunted the fact that Victor had saved her." Eli shook his head. "He didn't flinch. A smug expression came over his face. He said, 'Well, that was a lot of effort for nothing.' I asked him what he meant."

Eli's mouth twisted in a tormented grimace. "He said, 'As soon as you left her this evening, my guys found her. They finished the job I left undone.'"

"I didn't want to believe him, but the truth was in his eyes. I attacked him. I got a few good licks in, but the old man was… is… much stronger than I am. He beat the hell out of me. Left me lying on the floor."

He went to the liquor cabinet and poured another scotch, downed it in one gulp. "Once I came to, I went to find Christelle. She was gone. I don't know what he did with her body, but he murdered her."

Chills washed over her skin.

When he spoke, his voice sounded like it came from the grave. "This time, your father wasn't around to save her."

She stood. Her knees weakened, and she had to steady herself. She laid a gentle hand on his forearm. "I am so, so sorry."

Blinking rapidly, he cleared his throat. "I left the asshole. Left the EO's. After that, Victor took me in. And, well, you know the rest."

He met her gaze. Moisture glinted in his silver eyes.

She rested a hand on his jaw. "I'm sorry," she

whispered again.

He closed his eyes and turned his lips into her hand, placed a gentle kiss on her palm. She took his head in her hands and lifted. Saying nothing, she gently stroked his jaw, then touched her lips to his. He let out a soft groan. Cupping her face in his hands, he kissed her back, drove his tongue deep in her mouth. Her legs quivered. She nearly melted to the floor. This was wrong... dangerous. Eli was not the man for her... But God, it felt so...

He broke away and released her. "I'm... sorry. I shouldn't have done that."

She brought her hand to her lips and released a shaky laugh. "No, it's okay. I think maybe I did that." Her face burning, she grabbed her purse. "It's late. I'd better go."

He crossed his arms and gave a jerky nod. "Let me see you home."

"I can see myself home. Thanks, though. Thanks for the great dinner, the gift." She paused and bit her lip. "And, for telling me about Christelle. I know that was hard for you. I hope you feel better."

His mouth twisted into a parody of a smile. "Yeah, loads better."

She offered a return smile. "Well, good night then."

He lifted strands of hair from her shoulder and rubbed them between his fingers. His eyes captured hers, and a shudder ran through her body. "Good night, Liberty Van Helsing. Sweet dreams."

****

The weather was perfect the night of the party. A cool evening breeze blew, just enough to bring the smell of the ocean. Beyond the blue-green water, mystical dark clouds hovered over purple mountain peaks.

Colored lights were strung around a pavilion where a crowd had already gathered. Music blared from speakers. Liberty grimaced. *Please don't let them play "All About that Bass."*

Most of her friends were here. She wished Hannah could have made it, but she was spending most of her time at the hospital with her grandfather. He was improving, but slowly.

A large white banner with pink and purple lettering hung between two bamboo poles at the edge of the structure, spelling out 'Happy Nineteenth, Liberty. We Love You.'

Neal had definitely gone all out. Now that they'd reschedule the event to the night before the full moon, she was secretly thrilled. In spite of her new friends, she'd been lonely for family, lonely for her old life. Having a birthday party with her mother around was awesome.

Danielle and Neal greeted her as soon as she entered the pavilion. Her mom wore a figure flattering dress of soft peach. Her blonde hair was swept back in an elegant updo. She looked amazing.

Her mother took Liberty's hands and swept a gaze over her form-fitting mid-thigh lemon yellow dress. "You look beautiful," she whispered tearfully. She gently tucked Liberty's hair behind her ear. "I can't believe my little girl is all grown up. Where did the time go?"

Liberty hugged her and in that moment, didn't feel grown up at all. She felt like a little girl again. Safe. Loved.

They pulled apart, and Danielle frowned. "Are you really going to stay here on the island? You've been here long enough. Come home with me, please?"

How could she tell her she couldn't leave? That her destiny was to be a hunter? That she'd stepped into a life she couldn't turn her back on? "I miss you more than you could know, Mom. But I can't leave. This is my home now."

"How can it be your home when you've only been here a few months?"

She shrugged. "I can't explain it. I just know that I have to stay."

Her mother nodded, her mouth tight, and wiped away tears.

Neal cleared his throat. "Come on, pretty lady. Tonight is not the night for crying. How about a dance?"

"Memories" by Elvis filled the air, and Danielle smiled. "What a fitting song." She looked at Liberty. "Do you mind, dear?"

"Of course not, I should mingle."

Neal whisked Danielle away, and she laughed like a young girl. As much as Liberty disliked Dufus, she was glad to see her mom happy.

Ryan and Jenna stood together… close together. She was laughing at something he said. He looked down at her intently, as if she were imparting the secrets of the universe.

An ache spread from Liberty's heart to her stomach. What was wrong with her? She should want Ryan to be with someone. *She* was the one who chose to let him go. But, the truth was, seeing him look at Jenna like that was painful. She tightened her hands into fists and spun around.

Eli stood behind her, so close she almost bumped into him. She scowled. "I hate it when you do that."

He nodded toward Ryan. "I see lover boy's moved on already."

"It appears so."

"I don't get it. I thought you two had gotten past my mesmerizing him not to love you."

"We did get past it. Things just… didn't work out for us."

He pursed his lips. "Hmmm… well, I guess that's good, since we kissed."

Her face heated. "That was just a… moment. We agreed it shouldn't have happened, so can we just forget about it?"

He lifted his shoulders and let them drop. "I don't know, my kiss is pretty powerful. Since you can't be mesmerized, I doubt if *you* can forget about it."

She curled her nose up. "Whatever." *Jerk.* Hopefully, he didn't know how close to the truth he'd come.

He inclined his head toward Ryan and Jenna. "I see he's already found a replacement. You okay with that?"

She shrugged. "Of course I am. I'm completely over him." Ugh… why was she discussing her feelings for Ryan with Eli?

"If you're over him, what are the little green sparks shooting from your eyes?"

She tightened her mouth. "I'm not jealous. I'm glad he's found someone."

Eli leaned close and whispered, "Liar, liar, pants on fire."

His warm breath caressed her skin sending, sparks of electricity through her body. She edged back. "Stop it."

A waiter passed with a drink-laden tray, and Eli

snagged a glass of white wine and handed it to her. "Here. You look like you need this. Down it, and I'll take you out on the dance floor. We'll make him jealous."

She took a sip and snorted a laugh. "I'm not into childish games. I don't want to make him jealous."

He tutt-tutted. "Now, now. Didn't you know? Games of the heart are never childish." He snatched the glass from her and set it on a nearby table. "Come on, I'll hold you really close. We'll pretend we can't get enough of each other."

She tensed. Not a good plan... Judging by the effects of his kiss, maybe she *couldn't* get enough of him. But she didn't want to go down that road again. It was too treacherous and nothing but heartbreak waited at the end. She started to protest, but Eli swept her into his arms and onto the dance floor while Ed Sheeran serenaded them with "One."

Eli hadn't lied. He held her so closely; a slip of paper wouldn't fit between them.

"How's this?" His words vibrated against her ear. He brushed a thumb over her bare shoulder, and she forgot how to breathe.

"Nice," she whispered.

This was dangerous, foolish, and still, she pushed everything out of her mind. Forced herself to relax, let the music soothe her, give in to the sensation of being held by Eli.

He rested his forehead against hers. "Do you think it's working?"

"Hmmm?" She frowned. "Working? What...?"

Oh yeah, making Ryan jealous...

Eli peered across the dance floor. "He's glaring this way, and he looks pissed." He brought his attention back to her. "I think we fooled him." His voice dropped to a husky whisper, and the silver in his eyes shifted to molten gray.

Tremors racing over her skin, she spoke around the knot in her throat. "Yeah, we fooled him."

His hand on her back moved lower. His fingers spread, his palm pressing her closer… His steps slowed, and he tilted his head forward. He was going to kiss her again. And she wanted him to. She didn't care who was watching. She released a soft sigh and parted her lips.

His body tensed, and he glanced over her shoulder. A muscle ticked in his clenched jaw and, with a curt nod, he released her. She bit back a cry of frustration, shivering at the sudden loss of warmth.

"Liberty?"

She whirled to find Ryan behind her and brought a hand up to her chest to still her racing heart. "Hi, Ryan. Where's your date?"

"She's not my date."

"No? You two seemed pretty cozy."

He grimaced. The ever-present smile in his dark eyes was absent. "Not as cozy as you and Eli. I know it's not my business, that we're not together, but, are you two…?"

She looked back at Eli. He met her gaze, then said to Ryan, "No, dude, we aren't anything. Just pals."

She smiled brightly, in spite of the pang in her chest. "That's right. Just pals."

****

Breathless, Bianca left the dance floor. She hadn't taken a break since the party started. Her feet were killing her.

Chris Farmer, a guy she went out with a few times,

approached before she'd gone more than a few steps. "Wanna dance?"

She grimaced. "Sorry, love. I've got to rest. Catch me later?"

He frowned. "You sure?"

"Quite. See ya a bit later."

On the way to the bar, she stopped to slip off her heels, carrying them loosely in her fingers.

Jonathan, a bartender from Perfect Getaway, was mixing drinks.

She rested an elbow on the bar. "I'll have a double vodka soda with lime."

"Coming right up."

A male voice spoke from behind her. "Whiskey."

Bianca turned to find Diego standing next to her. His skin looked even more gray and parched than it had last time she'd seen him. Irritation flitted through her. "So…" She glanced around and lowered her voice. "I take it Nadia still isn't letting you feed?"

Diego cut her a look, then took the whiskey from the bartender and swallowed it in one gulp. He slammed the glass down and grabbed her arm.

She gasped. "What the hell are you doing?"

"Is everything okay?" Jonathan asked.

"Fine," Bianca called over her shoulder, then muttered under her breath, "I hope."

Diego didn't stop until they were in the copse of trees lining the beach.

She jerked away, rubbing her arm, and bent to slip on her shoes. "What do you think you're doing?"

"You need to watch what you say. Not everyone knows about vampires."

"Jonathan does. He's a local. I spoke quietly."

"That new guy, Neal, was nearby."

"Sorry. I didn't see him. But did you have to drag me away like some kind of caveman?"

He scrubbed his hands over his face. "I wasn't sure what else you'd say. I'm not exactly thinking straight these days."

"You look like shit. You have *got* to feed."

"I'll be fine."

She crossed her arms over her chest and huffed out a breath. "I don't get it. Why do you let her control you like that? What has she got on you? You're not a wuss. I just don't understand."

His jaw tightened, and he planted his hands on his hips, looking down at the ground. After a few moments, he lifted his head. "My father cheated on my mother their entire marriage. His commitment meant nothing to him. Between that and the abuse, he killed her. I swore I'd never cheat, never break a commitment."

"So you're just going to let her lead you around by the nose, eventually kill you?"

"No. If things don't change soon, I'm ending it. I just…" He heaved a sigh. "I just need to know I gave it my best shot."

She grunted a humorless laugh. "I'd say dying for her is giving it a pretty good shot." She shook her head. "You're an idiot." She whirled and headed back to the bar. She needed another double. Maybe a triple.

****

"Can I talk to you?" Ryan's gaze went to Eli then back to Liberty. "Alone?"

"Sure," Liberty said.

"Don't mind me." Eli cocked an eyebrow. "I'll just be here, fighting off all the women."

Ryan gave a derisive grunt and led her into a quiet corner.

She crossed her arms. "What's up?"

He studied her face. "I just want you to know that there's nothing between me and Jenna."

"Yes, you told me you weren't on a date."

"We aren't. But it's not because of how I feel about you."

She lifted her brows. "It's not?"

"No. I still love you, but I'm not going to sit around and pine for you. I like Jenna, as a friend. But I just thought you should know, if I meet someone I want to pursue a relationship with, I'm going to do that. In spite of how I feel about you."

She wanted to tell him not to, to wait for her, but that wouldn't be fair. "I understand, and you should. I hope you find someone." He was a good guy. He deserved an epic love. But until she sorted out her life—her destiny as a hunter, her feelings about Eli—she couldn't get involved with anyone.

"But if you decide you want me again, you'll let me know?" He grinned, his chocolate eyes crinkling at the corners, dimples creasing his cheeks.

She sighed. God, she loved those dimples…

Squeezing his hand, she smiled back. "You'll be the first."

He opened his mouth, but before he could speak, a scream ripped through the night.

Chapter 10

Liberty whirled. A colony of bats flew in, swarming toward party guests, who dove to the ground.

"Shit." Not holding the party on a full moon night hadn't done any good. The vampires had arrived.

Panicked, she searched the beach for her mother and spotted her ten feet away in Neal's arms. They cowered on the sand.

Liberty ducked low and hurried over to them. "You have to go. Hurry!"

Her mother raised a stricken expression. "You're coming with us."

"I can't."

"I'm not leaving without you." Danielle's voice shook, and tears streamed down her face.

Eli appeared behind them, grabbed Neal's arm, and practically lifted him off the ground. He caught and held Neal's gaze. "You'll get her out of here. Now. Take her home and lock the doors." His focus latched onto Danielle just as she opened her mouth to protest. "You'll go with him, quickly, quietly. And you'll both forget the vampires arriving and everything that happened after."

Neal nodded and slipped his arm around Danielle. They fled, running together. Liberty watched until they were a safe distance away. Thank God. She didn't have to worry about her mother… only the other fifty people under attack.

She hadn't brought her bow, but her gun and knife were never far. She lifted her skirt and jerked the Glock from the strap around her thigh.

Loud creaking noises rose above the din. Where once there were a horde of bats, at least a few dozen vampires now stood. People tried to flee, but several were grabbed by vampires.

To her left, Trey clutched a terrified, screaming woman. He bit into her neck. Blood poured onto the ground. Liberty fired and hit him in the shoulder. He spun, clutching his arm. The woman fell.

He squinted at Liberty and smiled. She and Trey had had run-ins before. The last time, he'd attacked Hannah and Liberty had fired at him and missed. Not this time…

He stalked toward her, one hand on his bleeding shoulder. She aimed for his heart. Before she could squeeze the trigger, he darted and was no longer in front of her. She searched through the chaos. A shiver rolled over her skin. Not having Trey in her sights made her nervous.

Ryan.

Where was Ryan? She spotted him several feet away, struggling with a female vampire. Ryan was strong, but he was no match for the strength of vampires… even a woman. The heavy-set purple-haired girl sank her fangs into his neck.

Liberty rushed toward them, gun drawn. Before she could reach them, someone grabbed her from behind. She caught a glimpse of Trey from her peripheral. He snatched her up by the shoulders and tossed her in the air. She landed hard on her back. Spots danced in front of her eyes, and her head swam. Darkness squeezed against her vision. *Don't pass out, Ryan needs you, don't*

114

pass out…

****

Bianca hid behind the bar, her legs shaking, tears running down her face. A few feet away, Chris lay, his throat torn out. What little blood that hadn't been drained from him trickled onto the sand. She bit her lip and closed her eyes. She was terrified, but her friends—her brother—needed her. They were out there, battling vicious vampires while she cowered like a gutless rabbit.

She glanced around for a weapon. The bar had been smashed. Chunks of wood lay scattered about the sand. Crouching, she scooted over and searched the debris. She snatched up a long, jagged piece of wood. Not the most effective weapon, but it would have to do. She ripped a piece of chiffon from her skirt and wrapped the handle of the makeshift stake.

She scanned the party area. It looked like a war zone. She couldn't see Liberty. But surely her friend was fine. She was a vampire hunter. She could hold her own.

Bianca found Diego, and a gasp left her throat. Two vampires circled him. Diego held a long-bladed knife, turning slowly, keeping his eyes on both of them. One of them lunged. Diego struck out with the knife, but the vampire overpowered him. The knife fell harmlessly to the ground. The other closed in.

"No!" Bianca screamed and ran. She lifted the stake, whacking the nearest vampire on the side of the head. With a growl, he stumbled back from Diego. She plunged the wood into the other vampire's back. He howled and whipped around. Oh God, had she missed his heart? Her knees shook, and she backed up a few steps. Time stalled in a long tortuous moment. Then his body jerked, and he toppled to the ground, writhing, bubbling to cinders.

Diego surged to his feet. "Bianca? Get the hell out of here. You'll get yourself killed."

She snorted. "Looks like I'm faring better than you."

Diego started to reply, then horror overtook his expression. The first vampire had recovered. He leapt on Bianca. The impact knocked the breath from her. He opened his mouth, his fangs protruding, and bent toward her. A sharp pain pierced her neck. She shrieked and tried to shove him off. He didn't budge. She struggled harder, screaming and pummeling his shoulders and chest with her fists. A ferocious growl rumbled the ground. He was lifted off her and tossed to the sand.

Diego snatched up the knife and drove it into the vampire's throat. He staggered back, clawing at the blade. Recovering quickly, Bianca tossed the stake to Diego. He caught it and staked the vampire through the heart.

Diego panted, trying to catch his breath. He swayed and peered at her through narrowed eyes. "Are you okay?" His voice was low, weak.

Bianca rose to her feet and brought a hand up to her neck. It came away bloody. But surprisingly, the pain was moderate. The vampire hadn't taken much of her blood. Her throat seemed still in one piece, unlike poor Chris. She shuddered. "Yeah, I'm good. What about you?"

Diego's lips tightened. "I'm fine. Useless, but fine."

"That's because you haven't had human blood. Nadia almost got you killed."

He shook his head. "No, it was me. I allowed her to weaken me."

"That's right." She cupped his jaw and turned him

to face her. "You have to feed."

His mocha eyes latched onto her neck. "I know."

Her heart skittered. She moistened her lips. "Go ahead," she whispered. "Feed on me."

His gaze met hers then moved back to her neck where blood dribbled. His face tightened. His eyes reddened. "I—I can't. You've been through enough tonight. I…"

Bianca brushed her hair back from the other side of her neck, where the vampire hadn't bitten her, and stepped closer to him. "Take it," she whispered.

His eyes glittered, and he dipped his head. His arms went around her. He pulled her tightly to his body. She gasped at the contact.

He held her gaze for a brief moment, then his teeth pierced the flesh on her neck. The difference between Diego and the other vampire was tremendous. Just a sting, then a warm rush of pleasure sweeping through her. Not a stab of pain, no fear.

A low, satisfied moan left his throat, trembling against her skin where his mouth drank from her. Each tug of his lips sent a rush of heat coursing through her body. She clutched his shoulders, holding on, afraid her knees would buckle.

A slow, sweet lethargy stole through her. Her head swam. She was light and she was floating… floating away into the sky…

Oh God, he was draining her!

"Diego, stop! You need to stop now." He kept drinking. "Diego, please!" She shoved against his shoulders, but his grip steeled until she thought he would crush her spine. "Diego!" she whimpered. "Please…" Darkness crowded her vision. She was slipping…

Suddenly, she was free. Her vision cleared.

Diego stood back, his mouth bloody, staring at her in horror. "Bianca?"

She blinked, wanting to speak, but not having the strength.

"I'm sorry." His face reset to its normal shade, eyes once more chocolate brown, the red completely faded. He skimmed his fingers along her cheek. "Please tell me you're okay." He scooped her into his embrace and cradled her against his chest. "I'll find Liberty. We'll get you taken care of."

She lifted her arms and wound them around his neck. Her vision was coming back, her mind clearing. "I—I'm okay."

His worried gaze searched her face. "Are you sure?"

She nodded. "I'm sure. I feel fine. You can put me down."

He held her more tightly to him. "I almost drained you."

"But you didn't. My strength is coming back." She studied his face and smiled. "And you look like you're doing better than you have in a while."

One side of his mouth lifted in a grin. "Yeah. Your blood is… delicious."

A shiver ran through her. What was wrong with her that a vampire feeding from her would be so… sensual? That she'd get a thrill of delight from his liking the taste of her blood? She cleared her throat and swallowed. "Please. Set me down."

He eased her to her feet. "You're sure you're okay?"

"Yes." She glanced around at the mayhem, the bodies, the destruction. A sob caught in her throat. "I just… it's so horrible."

"I know. I'm sorry. If I had been… myself, I could have stopped a lot of this. I'll never let Nadia dictate who I can feed on again."

Disappointment coursed through her, although she wasn't sure why. Just because she'd fed him, and they'd seemed to share a brief connection, it didn't mean that Nadia's hooks were no longer imbedded. "So, you're staying with her?"

He narrowed his eyes. "Is there a reason why I shouldn't?"

Other than that she's a raging bitch, not one I can think of. Aloud, she said. "I suppose not. As long as you guys are happy. None of my business."

Diego gave a curt nod. "Right. None of your business. Let's go check on the others."

****

Liberty lay still for a few moments, blinking back darkness, trying to catch her breath. She had no time for this. Ryan needed her. She shot a glance to where he still struggled with the vampire. Shit! She'd drain the life from him. She struggled to rise.

Eli swooped in and jerked the girl off of Ryan. Lifting her in the air, he drove his hand into her chest and ripped her heart out.

Liberty snapped her gaze away, bile rising.

Trey leaped on her before she could come to her feet. He straddled her and held her shoulders to the ground. His face hovered above her, longish dark hair swinging over his face.

She gripped her knife and jerked it from its sheath. Brought it up and plunged it into Trey's ribs. He grunted and laughed at the same time.

"You're a worthy adversary, Liberty Van Helsing."

Panting rapidly, he grimaced and tugged the knife from his flesh, then held it above her face. Blood dripped onto her skin, and she gagged. "I'll enjoy destroying you."

"Give it your best shot, asshole." She tightened her lips, pretending the blood wasn't making her want to hurl. She stretched her hand out to the side, searching for anything to grasp as a weapon. Her fingers closed over something… a broken bottle… She gripped the neck and swung upward, clipping him on the chin. Not enough to knock him out, but enough to catch him off guard. He grabbed his face, and she took the opportunity to buck and unseat him. Scrambling to her feet, she quickly wiped the blood off her face, her gaze sweeping the ground for her lost gun.

A roar sounded, and she raised her head. Trey was upon her, reaching out—

From her left, something flashed, and Trey went airborne. Eli had him by the throat, the two of them suspended midair before they landed on the ground with a thud.

Eli punched him, and Trey flew back, then recovered and came at him. He slammed his fist into Eli's jaw, and Eli stumbled, but remained on his feet.

With an inhuman growl, Eli launched at Trey and drove him into the ground. He straddled him, drew his hand back as if to drive it into his chest. Trey's form wavered, and a squeaking sound rose. He morphed into a bat, and Eli was left holding nothing. Trey flew into the night.

"Son of a bitch!" Eli came to his feet and looked back at her. "Are you okay?"

She shoved a handful of hair off her face and nodded. "I'm fine." Around the area, half a dozen party guests lay still, bleeding. Tears rose to her throat. She jerked her gaze away from the sight of their bodies.

A group of vampires stalked through the pavilion, overturning tables.

"You need to get out of here," Eli shouted. "I've got this."

She shook her head. "I'm not leaving. Not until they're gone."

He grabbed her arms. "I don't have time to look out for you. Get the hell out. Now!"

She jerked from his hold. "People are dying while we're standing here arguing. Let me do my job."

He let out a growl, his jaw so tight she thought it might shatter. Before he could say more, two vampires dove on top of him, driving him into the ground. He elbowed one, sending the vampire through the air. Eli jumped to his feet and threw a knife at the remaining vampire. The vampire gasped and grabbed the blade protruding from his chest, then toppled to the ground. Liberty darted to help Eli. Something hit her from behind. She went down, head spinning.

She turned to find a female vampire, blonde hair wild around her head, fangs bared. The vampire lunged toward her.

Liberty drew back her fist and punched her in the jaw. The vampire's head jerked back, and she stumbled away with a shriek. In seconds, she found her footing and came at Liberty again. The blonde whipped a knife out of her boot and thrust it forward. Searing, burning pain ripped through Liberty's arm. She felt the sticky rush of blood, but couldn't look at it. If she did, she would be done.

Gritting her teeth, Liberty sucked air in through her

mouth. When the vampire came at her again, she side-stepped and dropped into a squat, at the same time, grabbing a broken chair leg. One end came to a slanted point. Maybe not sharp enough to pierce the vampire's skin, but she had to take a shot.

With another shriek, the vampire ran toward her. Liberty thrust the stake out and plunged it into her chest. The vampire drew in a gasp and came to a halt. Her eyes widened, her mouth stretched into a grimace, and she thumped to the sand. Her body shriveled and smoldered into ash.

Liberty surveyed the area. Eli stood over the body of a vampire. A few humans staggered away, their arms wrapped around one another. From a distance, came the wail of an ambulance. Hopefully, the casualties would be few.

Eli's expression was ferocious as he headed toward her. "You're hurt," he bit out.

She tried to laugh, to tell him she was fine, but the sound caught in her throat. Burning, agonizing pain, oddly tinged with numbness, screamed through her arm. She glanced down. *Big mistake*. A sea of red gushed from a gash in her bicep. Nausea cramped her stomach, rose to her throat. Her head spun, and large black dots swarmed her vision.

"Eli, I…" She slumped, barely aware of him shooting across the distance that separated them. His strong arms scooped her up, then everything went black.

Chapter 11

Liberty's eyes fluttered open… she was floating… how could that be…? She came fully awake just as Eli carried her through the door of the Van Helsing mansion.

Antoine hovered in the foyer. "What happened?"

"Fucking vampires," Eli snapped.

"I thought *you* were a fucking vampire."

Eli's mouth quirked. "Funny, old man. They attacked the party. She took a knife to the arm. She's going to bleed out if we don't do something."

Her head swam, and her mouth felt like she'd swallowed cotton, but she croaked out, "I'm fine."

Eli snorted. "You almost died."

"Put me down. I can walk. I just need to go to bed."

Eli released her so abruptly, she swayed. She grasped the arm of the sofa and slowly lowered.

"You need to have that looked at." Eli's voice was tight with annoyance.

Antoine frowned. "Let me see." He sat next to her.

She rolled up her sleeve, and Antoine took hold of her arm. Shooting pain traveled up through her shoulder. She winced.

"That hurts?"

She twisted her mouth. "No, it felt good. Why don't you do it again?"

His frown turned into a scowl. "Sarcasm does not become you. I will tend to it. I do not believe it needs stitches."

Eli folded his arms over his chest, his jaw taut, while Antoine disappeared.

She looked up at him. "I'm okay. You can go now."

He shook his head. "So that's the thanks I get for saving your ass?"

"I appreciate it. Really, I do. I'm just saying. I'm fine. You don't have to hang around."

"I'll wait and make sure he gets you taken care of. Make sure you get to bed okay."

She pictured Eli, 'getting her to bed,' and her breath caught. She tugged her eyes away from his intense gaze and swallowed loudly. "I don't understand. If the EO's want to keep a low profile, why would they stage such a public attack?"

"Rupert sometimes enjoys a spectacle where he can flex his muscles. Most of the attendees were locals. They, the authorities, and the media will cover up the truth. If a few tourists survived and claim a vampire attack, who would believe them?"

"So, Rupert can choose to slaughter at will, but unless he orders it, the vampires have to keep a low profile?"

Eli grinned. "Pretty much."

Antoine returned with a medical kit and a glass of water. He shook out a few pills from a bottle and held them out, along with the water. "Here you go, Miss Liberty."

She squinted at him. "What are they?"

He smirked. "Arsenic, what do you think?"

Eli chuckled. "They're pain pills, dummy. Just take them."

"Will they make me feel funny?"

"They will make you feel better." Antoine dropped them into her hand. "Just take them."

She swallowed the pills, and Antoine laid a towel under her arm. Without warning, he poured antiseptic over the wound. Fire sizzled her skin. "Ouch!"

"Sorry miss, it has to hurt to heal."

She tightened her mouth. "I just wasn't expecting it to hurt that much."

He frowned down at her arm. "Maybe you should be seen after all. It is deeper than I first suspected."

She shook her head. "It's not necessary."

Antoine gave a curt nod. He added ointment to the wound and wrapped a bandage around it. His ministrations, along with the pills were already working. The pain eased and her limbs relaxed. "Thanks. Much better."

She stood, and her head swam with dizziness. She eased back down onto the sofa. "Whoa."

"Are you all right?" Antoine's brows creased.

"Just a little dizzy. I'm not used to drugs."

He nodded. "Probably had something to do with the blood loss too."

"Come on. I'll help you upstairs." Eli reached out a hand.

"I'm fine. I can make it." She rose again, slowly this time.

Eli huffed out a breath and swept her into his arms. "Damn stubborn…"

"Put me down!"

"He will put you down upstairs, Miss Liberty. Please do not argue. It is late and I, for one, would like to retire."

She clamped her lips together. "Sorry we disturbed

you, Antoine. Thank you."

He inclined his head. "My pleasure."

Eli strode from the room and took the stairs two at a time, with her still in his arms. He kicked her bedroom door open and dropped her onto the bed.

She harrumphed. "Wow. Your chivalry leaves me breathless."

"I figure you want me out of here as soon as possible."

"That's right. I do."

He paced away from her, then back. He opened his mouth, clamped his lips together, shook his head. He lifted a hand and let it drop. "Forget it," he snarled, then strode through the door and slammed it shut.

"Good riddance," she muttered, and tried to ignore the pain that squeezed her heart.

****

Liberty relaxed against the towel, letting the sun warm her, soothe her. After last night, she needed some relaxation.

"You okay, love?" Bianca's drowsy voice came from beside her.

"I'm fine. Just a little sore. How about you?"

"Truth be told, a bit shaken up. You might be used to that sort of melee, but for me, it was slightly traumatic."

Liberty opened one eye and glanced at Bianca's neck. "I'm just grateful they didn't drain you when they fed on you. Especially since it appears more than one attacked you."

Bianca shrugged. "Thankfully, Diego rescued me."

"From both vampires?"

"Well…" Red colored her tanned complexion.

"Actually, Diego was the second one to feed on me."

"What?" Liberty bolted to a sitting position, all thoughts of relaxation forgotten. "Diego fed on you?"

"It's no big deal."

"No big deal? *Right*. You have a thing for Diego, he's with Nadia, yet last night he rescues you *and* feeds on you? Come on, spill."

Bianca sat up as well. She swept a handful of dark hair back from her face and sighed. "The story is not all that titillating. Nadia has been a bitch and won't let him feed. He agreed not to feed on another human other than her, but she withholds her blood like some sort of sadistic torturer." She scooped sand up and spread her fingers, watching it fall. "Last night, he was so weak, he could barely defend himself." She looked out over the water. "So I offered to let him feed."

"Oh wow." No matter how frightening the prospect, Liberty couldn't help but harbor a strange desire to know what it would feel like to have someone, other than a violent psycho vampire, feed on her. "Was it… sexy?"

Bianca scowled. "Sexy?"

"Sure. Come on, the act is just a little intimate, wouldn't you say? Especially if there's an attraction."

Bianca brushed off her hands and lay back down. Her disgustingly incredible figure was even more perfect in the lime green bikini she wore. Liberty resisted the urge to cover up with a towel.

"Truthfully?" A smile curved Bianca's lips. "Yes. It was a bit exciting."

Liberty laughed. "I knew it!" She squelched a sudden rush of envy. She would never feel that kind of intimacy, Eli would never be able to feed on her.

"Yes, well. So much for that. He's with Nadia. He's

whipped."

"He'll wise up eventually. Hopefully, sooner than later." Liberty lay down on her blanket and accidently put her weight on her injured arm. "Ouch! Damn."

Bianca's forehead scrunched in concern. "What is it?"

"Just this damn arm. Hurts like a bitch."

"Why don't I work for you this evening? You need a night off. Especially since you have the hunt coming up."

"I appreciate it, but this is your only day off."

"No. I insist. You can work for me some other time."

"Are you sure?"

"Absolutely."

"Okay, I accept. Thanks. I can take Hannah to visit her grandparents at the hospital."

Bianca snorted a laugh. "So much for taking a night off to chill. Are you in competition for some kind of sainthood medal?"

Liberty scrunched her nose. "Haha." She shook her head. "I just feel awful for them. Hannah will be all alone if something happens to her grandparents."

Bianca grinned. "No, she won't, love. She'll have you."

****

Bianca gathered condiments from her tables and loaded them onto trays. Thankfully, the tiki bar was closed. Now she just had to finish her side work. What was she thinking, offering to cover Liberty's shift? She must be daft. Her gaze cut to Diego behind the bar. Damn… He was the real reason she'd offered. She was becoming completely smitten with him. Most *definitely* daft.

128

She passed by the bar, holding a tray loaded down with condiments. Diego popped around and took them from her. "Let me help you with that."

She smiled. "Thank you."

"No problem." He carried the tray to the back, and she followed him.

To her surprise, he hung around and helped her fill the condiments.

"How've you been?" She glanced at him from the corner of her eyes. "Since the... blood. Is Nadia letting you feed on her?"

"I'm fine. And, no, she isn't. Your blood has seemed to sustain me."

A flush of pleasure warmed her skin. *Silly girl.* "If you need to... I mean, if you get hungry and she won't let you..."

He smiled. "Thanks. I might take you up on that." He capped the ketchups and let out a breath. "Nadia and I are over."

"You... you are?"

"Yeah. I got tired of her jerking me around. Besides, I didn't feel right about... you know."

"About feeding on me? That was completely innocent."

He gave her a lopsided grin. "Was it?" He capped the final bottle and crowded closer to her. "You didn't feel anything?"

Tingles skittered through her stomach. "Well, yes, I mean... it was... different."

"Exciting?" His low voice caressed her skin.

She couldn't speak, so she only nodded.

"Feeding can be just a normal activity for sustenance, if two people aren't attracted to one another.

If they are, well, it's a whole different story."

A breathless chuckle escaped. "And you think I'm attracted to you?"

He bent forward until their faces were millimeters apart. "You tell me."

"Well." Her voice came out in a husky rasp. "I… It's not like we… we kissed or anything."

"Hmmm… good point." His eyes caught hers, then dropped to her mouth. He bent his head, and his lips touched hers. Lightning zinged through her body. She opened her mouth, and his kiss deepened.

"Ah, excuse me." A voice came from the doorway. They jumped apart, and Bianca brought a hand to her mouth.

Jonathan stood inside the kitchen.

"Yeah, what is it?" Diego's tone was clipped, his breathing uneven.

"The hospital called. Your sister's been hurt."

Bianca gasped.

Diego's expression tensed. "Hurt? How badly?"

He shook his head. "I don't know. They said you should get there right away."

Bianca grabbed her purse from the cupboard. "I'm going with you." She jerked her apron off and threw it across the tray of condiments, knocking half of them askew.

Diego was gone in a flash. She rushed outside and jumped in his car before he took off.

Neither of them spoke as he sped to the hospital, not only breaking the speed limit, but perhaps the sound barrier.

He peeled into the hospital parking lot and vaulted from the car. Bianca raced to keep up with him and found him at the emergency room desk.

"Where is my sister?" He scrubbed his hands over his face. "Selena Ortega. She was brought in a few minutes ago."

The middle-aged woman behind the desk consulted a computer screen and looked up, sympathy in her expression. "Room five. Through there." She pointed to swinging doors with 'Emergency' lettered over the top.

Diego burst through the doors, Bianca following behind. He didn't seem aware she was even there, but she had to be. For Selena… and for him.

Diego's father was seated in a plastic chair in the hallway. He stood when Diego came in.

Diego glared at him. "What happened?"

Gerardo's face was drawn, and his lips quivered. "I don't know. She was in her room. I heard a crash. I raced upstairs, and she was lying on the floor. A chair was overturned. I think she was trying to hang something, and she fell."

"How is she?" Diego's voice shook.

"The doctor is with her now."

Doctor Lemanu came out from behind the curtain of room five. He frowned and looked from Diego to his father.

Diego grabbed his forearm. "How is she? What's wrong with her?"

The doctor gently shrugged loose. "She's injured pretty badly." He turned to Diego's father. "I understand she fell, Mr. Ortega?"

"That's right."

Footsteps pounded from behind. Bianca glanced over her shoulder. Liberty rushed up, green eyes dark with worry. "Bianca? What happened? I was with

Hannah. I heard they brought Selena in?"

Bianca nodded. "She… The doctor is explaining her condition."

Liberty took her hand and squeezed.

Doctor Lemanu's gaze pierced Gerardo. "Her injuries are pretty severe for a fall. She has a broken arm and three broken ribs. One of which has punctured a lung. Her jaw is dislocated."

Dread spiked Bianca's blood. She tightened her grip on Liberty's hand. *The son of a bitch…*

A strangled groan came from Diego. "My God… will she be okay?"

"It will take surgery to repair her lung and jaw. But she's in good hands."

Gerardo let out a sob. "It's all my fault. I should have hung the pictures for her. She'd been begging me to do it, and I kept putting it off. She was standing on a barstool, and she crashed into her dresser."

The doctor was silent for a moment, then slowly nodded. "I see."

A red haze of rage nearly blinded Bianca. "Bullshit!"

Everyone turned to look at her. Diego narrowed his eyes. "What?"

Bianca pointed a shaking finger at Diego's father. "He did it!"

Something shifted in Gerardo's expression. His haggard face went from concerned to angry. A glint of anger sparked in his hard eyes. "What the hell are you talking about?" He took a step toward her.

Bianca released Liberty's hand, but stood her ground. "You hurt her. I know you did."

Diego glanced at his father, then back to her. "The

doctor said it could have happened from a fall."

"Could have, but didn't." Bianca gripped his arm. "I need to talk to you." She pulled, and he followed her to the end of the hallway, out of earshot of the others. She released him and shoved her hair out of her face, crossing her arms over her chest. She looked up at him through tear filled eyes. "I know he did it."

"How are you so sure? I mesmerized him not to touch her."

"For some reason, it didn't work. Maybe because you were a new vampire, maybe because he was drunk at the time. Regardless, I know it didn't, because he hurt her just a few days ago."

His jaw tightened, and his dark eyes glittered dangerously. "He what?"

"When they came into the Getaway, I saw bruises on her arm." Bianca swallowed back tears. "I made her admit what happened. Your dad hit her."

"And you didn't tell me?" His words were a low growl.

Misery and guilt filled her soul. She shook her head. "Selena made me promise not to."

He grabbed her arms, his fingers digging painfully into her flesh. "I don't give a damn what you promised. You should have told me. Look what happened. You could have prevented it."

"She… she said if I told you, she'd kill herself. I checked on her every day after I found out. She seemed fine, so I didn't say anything. I couldn't risk her doing something to hurt herself." Her gaze searched his. "Don't you understand? I was trying to protect her."

"Protect her?" He barked a harsh laugh. "You did an *awesome* job." He shoved her away and shot down the hallway toward his father.

When Bianca reached them, Diego had his dad against the wall, his arm across his throat. "I'll rip your head off you sorry, pathetic coward."

His father's face reddened, and he gasped for air.

Bianca took hold of Diego's arm and tugged. "Stop, please, Diego. If you hurt him, Selena will never forgive you."

He tossed her away as if she weighed nothing. She stumbled back and banged painfully against the wall.

Liberty held out a hand. "Come on, Diego. Let him go. He's not worth it."

A commotion at the end of the hall drew Bianca's attention. Three security guards headed their way.

Diego's face tightened, and his eyes glowed red.

Bianca didn't see Gerardo move, but suddenly, he held a knife. He brought his arm up just as Liberty stepped between him and Diego. The knife caught her in the side. She cried out and slumped to the floor. Blood seeped through her white blouse.

"Oh my, God!" Bianca dropped to her knees. "Get a doctor, quick!"

Liberty winced. "It's just a nick."

Diego let out an inhuman growl and lifted his father in the air, threw him down the hallway where he landed with a bone jarring crack. Diego vaulted toward him. The three security guards tried to restrain Diego, but he tossed them off.

Doctor Lemanu squatted to check Liberty's wound. "She's fine. It's a surface wound." He motioned a nurse over. "Hauni, please take care of Miss Van Helsing."

Bianca and the nurse helped Liberty to her feet and into an empty room.

"Lay back, please." When Liberty obeyed, Hauni pushed her shirt back and swabbed the wound.

Bianca touched Liberty's cheek. "I'll be back, love."

"Go. I'll be fine."

Bianca hurried into the hall.

The security guards stood next to Diego. One had his hand on Diego's shoulder. "You okay, son?"

Diego nodded, but his face was strained with anger. His father was nowhere in sight. Thank God. No more violence. At least for the time being.

Diego looked up. Spotting Bianca, he walked away from the guards. She started toward him, but he held up a hand. "I'm going to see my sister. You need to leave."

Pain shafted through her heart. "Please, don't shut me out. I'm worried about her."

His dark eyes pierced her with anger. "You should have thought about that before you nearly got her killed."

A sob caught in her chest. "Diego, I'm sorry—"

"Enough! Get out of my sight. I might have to see you at work, but I don't have to look at you here."

Bianca froze, afraid to move or speak in case the dam of tears welling in her chest broke through. Diego disappeared into Selena's room, and on weighted feet, Bianca headed in to check on Liberty.

Chapter 12

Liberty pulled up at the house. *Shit*. Eli was on the porch, leaning against the railing.

She climbed reluctantly from her car. He straightened from his relaxed pose and bore down on her just as she reached the steps.

"Are you out of your mind?" His gaze dropped to her side. "How bad is it?"

"Not bad." She sighed wearily. "How did you know?"

"Word gets around." A muscle ticked in his jaw, and his eyes shot silver flames. "This is just the kind of thing I'm talking about."

"What?"

"Putting yourself in danger. Being so damn stubborn, you won't listen to anyone."

"I'm *really* not in the mood." She stalked past him and entered the silent house. He followed her up to her room.

"Seriously?" She spun around and slapped her hands on her hips. "It's been a long day."

"You almost got yourself killed."

"But I didn't, did I?"

"*This* time."

"Okay, okay. I get it. I'm taking too many risks. I'm stubborn and stupid and incompetent." Her eyes stung, and she blinked rapidly. "And I'm going to get myself killed, then there would be no Van Helsing to battle the EO's. Blah, blah, blah." She tossed her purse onto the chair. "Sorry. I'd hate for my death to screw things up for you."

His mouth quirked. "Yeah, I'd hate it too."

She twisted her lips into a sneer. "After all, that *is* the only reason you want me to stay safe. So I can hunt vampires."

His eyes narrowed. A glint of some emotion flickered and disappeared. He didn't reply.

"Well? That's right, isn't it? That's the only reason you worry about me?" She moved closer, and his body visibly tensed.

"What are you doing, Liberty?" His voice cracked. His Adams apple bobbed with an audible swallow.

"I'm simply asking you a question." She took another step and ran a finger down his taut arm. She was playing with fire, and she knew it. But she couldn't help herself. His moodiness, his evasiveness, his highhandedness were driving her crazy. It was time to get everything out in the open. "Is that it? Is that the reason you don't want anything to happen to me? Because I'm a Van Helsing, and the island needs me?" She waited, heart pounding.

His eyes dropped to her mouth. "This is ridiculous." His husky resonance encouraged her.

She chanced another step closer, until their bodies touched. She gazed up into his face and spoke softly. "Answer me."

Silence and heat pulsed between them. He stood immobile. Not speaking.

Really? Nothing? She forced a chuckle and moved away. "The big brave vampire is just a big fat chicken," she taunted. "You're afraid of me."

"I am *not* afraid of you."

She shook her head and turned her back on him. "Just forget abou—"

He grabbed her arm and spun her around to face him. She winced at the sting in her injured side, but he didn't apologize.

He gripped her shoulders and yanked her close. "You want an answer, Liberty? Do you? You got it. I don't worry about you because you're a hunter and the island needs you. I worry about you because I care. I care too damned much, and it sickens me. The thought of anything happening to you, of you being hurt, or killed, is like having a stake driven through my heart."

Her breath tripled. Looking into that molten silver gaze, suddenly, *she* was afraid of *him*. Afraid of the consequences of laying their feelings out. Terrified that the intensity, the fire, would singe her to ashes. She tried to pull away, but he held tight.

"We're not done." His growl sent bumps of awareness over her skin. "You asked and now you're going to listen."

"Eli—"

"I have feelings for you, Liberty. Strong feelings that I *hate*, with every molecule of my being. I hate that every time I see you, I want to grab you and kiss you and never let you go. The thought of you being with Ryan, of his touching you, of any man touching you drives me insane." His rapid breaths matched hers. "You know what I hate most of all? That no matter how I feel or how much I want you, *I can never have you*." His grip squeezed, shooting pain through her so deep, she couldn't tell if it was her side or her heart. He abruptly released her. His eyes flashed, and he gritted his teeth. "Is that what you wanted to hear? Are you happy now?"

She couldn't speak. Tears sprang to her eyes.

He grunted a humorless laugh and scraped a hand through his hair. "You wanted the truth and now you have it."

Her body trembled. Her skin burned like an inferno and froze, simultaneously. Oh God, this was it. It was now or never. "You can have me."

He drew in a sharp breath. "What?"

"Take me," she whispered. She cupped his face in her hands. Her eyes searched his. "I'm right here. And you can have me."

"We can't be together. You know that." The words were clipped, tense, as if he were holding himself in check.

"Maybe not forever. But just for now." She stood on tiptoe and gently pressed her lips to his. "We can have now, even if that's all we ever have."

He tensed, then with a groan, slid his arms around her, brought her tight against his body, bent his head and touched his lips to hers. His mouth was warm, firm, devouring her like he couldn't get enough. Her tongue met his, savoring and searching. She wanted closer to him, to draw him into her, mesh her body with his.

His hands caressed her hips, held her to him. His erection pressed against her abdomen, igniting a spark of both fear and excitement.

He broke away. His breath was ragged, eyes half closed. "Liberty… I…if we don't stop…"

She gripped his shirt and tugged him closer. "Please don't stop."

With only the slightest hesitation, his lips locked on

hers once more. Mouths fused, he scooped her into his arms and stalked to the bed, lowered her to the mattress. He followed, running his hands over her butt, her hips, her breasts. He lifted his mouth from hers to kiss her neck. Warm breath heated her skin, sent a shiver through her blood. She was burning up, drowning, spiraling all at the same time. She fumbled with the buttons on his shirt. He kissed her neck, working down to her chest, to the vee in her shirt, dipping his mouth in her cleavage. His lips were hot, firm, trailing a blaze so intense, she thought she would ignite.

She finally got his shirt undone and pushed it from his shoulders. He shrugged it off. His fingers went to the buttons of her blouse. She ran her hands over firm pecs. His cool skin was smooth, yet hard. Her fingers explored. She couldn't get enough of touching him.

He opened her blouse and ran his lips over her breast, through her lacey bra. His tongue skimmed her nipple, and heat rushed to her center. Pressing her lower body against his, she strained against him. "Oh, God. Eli… I want you…" she murmured.

He lifted his head to stare into her face. "I've wanted you for so long." He caressed her breast with his hand, then ran his fingers down her stomach, stopping at the waist of her sweats. He kissed her again, dipped his head and licked her other nipple. "You taste so…" He groaned. "Your skin is like satin."

Her muscles tightened. An urgent need gripped her… the need to get closer to him, as close as two people could get.

"Condom?" she panted. His touch made her insane with desire.

"I can't get diseases and, since we went through the

whole, *I can't give you a Van Helsing heir* thing, you know I can't get you pregnant, right?" His words, his mouth, teased her skin.

"Uh… oh, yeah. That. I'm just not… thinking very clearly."

His lips landed back on her throat. He drew in a deep breath. "I can smell your blood through your skin. Smells… delicious." He emitted a low, husky growl.

She pulled back. His face was gray, eyes blazing red. "Eli? You… you know you can't… drink me?"

He drew away. "Sorry." He squeezed his eyes shut. When he opened them, his face was back to normal. "I'm good now. Sorry."

She touched her lips to his. His tongue delved into her mouth, tangled with her tongue. She fumbled with the snap on his jeans. This time, he helped her. His hands covered hers, and they both unfastened his jeans. He tucked his hands in the waist of her sweats and pushed them down over her thighs. She kicked them off. Cool air kissed her skin. She pressed against him, groin to groin. The only things separating them were the lace of her panties and the boxer briefs he wore.

He cupped his hand on the back of her head and kissed her deeply, his lower body pressing against hers. He lifted his head a few inches. "Liberty…" His eyes were hooded, but she could see the question in them. "If you want to stop, now is the time. In a few seconds, I won't be able to."

She smoothed his hair back from his forehead and stared into his incredibly beautiful eyes. "No way in hell are we stopping."

He captured her mouth once more, while his hand worked her panties down. At the same time, she pushed his boxer briefs off his hips. They kicked their underwear aside, and he slid on top of her. Her mind was mush, her heart soaring and pounding out of her chest.

He stared down into her face, gently sweeping tendrils of hair off her cheeks, her forehead. "God, you're beautiful."

She laughed and kissed him. "I want you, Eli. Please. Now."

He groaned and closed his eyes, then opened them, staring into hers as he slowly, gently obeyed her command.

****

Son of a bitch. She was a virgin. *Was* being the key word. He'd taken something precious from her, even though he could offer nothing in return.

He sat up against the headboard and scrubbed his hands over his face. Dammit to hell. He was a bastard.

She lay with one hand under her soft cheek, lips curved in a slight smile. Moonlight cast gentle shadows on her skin. The necklace he'd given her nestled against her naked flesh. There'd been something so hot, yet profound, about loving her while her nude body was adorned with nothing except his gift… as though he'd marked her, branded her as his.

He ached to touch her again, to wake her and plunder her body once more, lose himself in her sweetness, her scent. In the two and a half centuries of his existence, he'd had countless women. Most had been nothing more than sexual partners. He'd loved Christelle. Had made love to her. But with Liberty… their joining had been beyond sex, beyond lovemaking. He'd been consumed—heart, mind, soul, and body. All the way. Forever.

Fuck. Dude, you are in so much trouble…

In spite of how much he wanted her, he never should have touched her. Nothing good would come of it. Crazy that he was going to have to hurt someone he'd willingly rip out his own heart to protect. But that was exactly what he had to do. Hurt her. Lie to her. Even if he couldn't lie to himself.

He slid out of bed and picked up his jeans from the floor. A soft sigh caught his attention. She'd shifted, the sheet tugging down to display the curve of one perfect breast. His muscles tightened. Heat and chills stirred in his groin. The jeans fell from his hands, and he crawled back into bed.

He wouldn't touch her again, wouldn't disturb her. But damned if he could make himself leave.

Fuck.

****

Liberty stretched and opened her eyes. The memories of last night flooded back, and she smiled. She turned to find Eli still lying next to her. "Good morning," she murmured.

"Morning." His silver eyes sparkled in the pre-dawn shadows. "Sleep well?"

"Amazing. You?"

"I don't sleep at night, remember?"

She frowned. "So, you stayed here all night, awake? What did you do?"

"Don't worry, I didn't stare at you the whole time like some creepy stalker."

She chuckled and stretched again. "That's comforting. Why didn't you leave?"

"I wanted to be with you. I knew this was our only time together. I didn't want it to end."

Her happiness deflated like a flat tire. "Our only time together?" She sat up and pulled the sheet over her breasts.

"Well, yeah. We agreed. We can't be together. We only had the one night."

A knot of pain formed in her throat, and she swallowed to keep the tears at bay. "Right."

"Are you okay with that?"

No. "Yes, sure. I just… I wasn't thinking past last night I guess."

He brushed hair back from her face and let his fingers linger against her cheek in a caress. "Why didn't you tell me you were a virgin?"

Her face heated, and she pulled away. "I didn't think it was important."

He expelled a loud breath. "A guy usually likes to know when he's a girl's first. I wouldn't have—"

"We wouldn't have made love if you'd known?"

A muscle ticked in his jaw and he looked away. "I don't know."

Irritation shot through her. "Sorry I didn't tell you so that you could have avoided something you obviously regret."

He brought his gaze back to her, his mouth quirking in a grin. "I don't regret it. Let's not ruin a perfect night by being a bitch this morning."

She tried to hold onto her anger, but a chuckle broke through. "You're right. *Let's* not be a bitch."

He smiled and threw the covers off and climbed from bed. Her heart skittered at the sight of his muscled, bare body. A flush warmed her cheeks, and she averted her face. God, she was totally *staring* at him.

"Don't worry, I'm dressing. You can stop with the

blushing, although I'll have to say, it's damned adorable."

She lifted her head. He was sliding into his jeans. Sparse dark blond hair on his chest and stomach, disappeared beneath the waistband of his jeans. He tugged his shirt on, but left it unbuttoned. His hair was mussed. *Damn.* Bed head looked really good on him.

"I need to go. Catch a few hours' sleep before tonight."

"Tonight?"

"Full moon, remember?"

"Oh yeah."

A frown creased his brow. "How's the injury?"

"Better."

He leaned down, and she turned her face up. His lips pressed gently against her forehead. Like he'd kiss a sister. It truly was over. They'd really just had the one night? She tried to tamp down her disappointment. Eli was a player. She knew he didn't do commitment. But just one night, really?

She didn't want to admit it to him, but her first time had been much, much more than she expected. At first, there had been a little pain, slight discomfort, then... magic. She'd never dreamed anything could feel so good, that she could feel so... complete.

Oh, geez. Was she pathetic or what? Screw it. She wouldn't let him know how she'd hoped this was the beginning of something special. That she wasn't just another girl he banged and ditched.

She forced nonchalance into her voice. "Well, okay then. This was... great. Thanks a lot. I guess I'll see you around."

He stared hard at her, then gave a brief nod. "Okay.

Right. I'll see you tonight."

She tightened her lips to keep from blurting out her feelings.

He walked out the door, and she threw herself back on the bed, pissed when errant tears escaped.

****

The night of the hunt, the town was deserted. A light sprinkle fell. Behind the curtain of mist, a full moon floated lazily in the dark sky. Liberty wandered down Main Street, snuggling her jacket more tightly around her when a chilly breeze blew over her damp skin.

Where were the vampires? Despite their unwelcome appearance the night of her party, she'd expected them out in full force. This was the only night of the month they could turn humans. If they were out, they were being discreet.

A handful of customers strolled in and out of Steamy Nights, one of the few businesses in Sang Croc that refused to close on full moon nights. Liberty pulled her cell from her pocket and checked the time. Two a.m. She'd been out since sundown. If nothing occurred in the next hour, she would give up, go home and climb in bed.

Her mind spun with thoughts of last night. She had given her virginity to Eli without a second thought. And, in spite of the way it ended, she wasn't sorry. Making love with him had been amazing. His touch was imprinted on her skin, on her heart. No matter what happened, she refused to regret giving herself to him. Was this what love felt like? If so, it was both euphoric and devastating.

She let out a groan of frustration. Restlessness and loneliness seized her. She wanted to text someone, wanted to do *something* to relieve the quiet. But everyone she knew was asleep. Except maybe Eli…

No. She wouldn't text him. She already thought about him more than she should, was more attracted to him than she should be. He preferred keeping her at a distance. She'd be damned if she'd let him know how much she cared… how *non*-distant she felt toward him. She'd rather walk on hot coals barefoot.

"Quiet night, huh?"

She jumped and whirled, jerking her bow to her shoulder.

Eli stood behind her, hands lifted. "Easy there, Barbie. It's just me, remember? Your friendly vampire?"

Her heart stalled, then pumped so fast she thought it would fly from her chest. She cleared her throat and took a deep breath to steady her nerves. "What the hell are you doing, sneaking up on me like that?"

He shrugged. "I didn't realize how trigger happy you were."

She lowered the bow. "So, I guess you turned someone already? Willing or no?"

Eli grunted a laugh. "I think questions like that are better left unanswered."

A chill slivered down her spine. Eli might be a 'good' vampire, but he still destroyed lives, killed people when the need arose. Then again, didn't she?

She rubbed her damp hands down the sides of her jeans. "Yeah, I don't even want to know."

He frowned and glanced around. "Have you seen any vampires out tonight?"

"No. Not one. Kind of odd, isn't it?"

"Yeah, it's odd. Freaky odd."

Dread washed over her. "You don't think it means…"

Eli grimaced. "If they're giving up turning, they're up to something."

Her eyes widened. "Hannah?" She jerked her phone out of her pocket and dialed Hannah's cell. It went straight to voicemail. She called the hospital.

The volunteer transferring her to Lester's floor took forever. Finally, his floor nurse answered.

"Is Hannah there?" The words tumbled out in a breathless gasp.

"She left earlier tonight. Said she was going home."

Liberty hung up and dialed the Van Helsing house phone. No answer. No Antoine.

She shoved her phone back into her pocket and raised her eyes to Eli. "Hannah…" She swallowed hard.

He frowned. "I'll drive."

Chapter 13

Liberty's stomach clenched with worry as she rode next to Eli. Had they taken Hannah? First her grandparents, then her?

Her mind whirred, trying to make sense of the vampires' absence. "Why wouldn't any of them have been out? If they're after Hannah, it wouldn't take all of them."

Eli glanced at her. "I'm sure a few were out, turning humans. But Rupert likes drama. The fact they kept a low profile could have been his way of sending you a message. Letting you uselessly wander around while they're…"

She was glad he didn't finish the sentence. Her guts were twisted up enough without hearing it said aloud.

He barely slowed before swerving into the Van Helsing driveway. Liberty jerked the car door open, but Eli was out and in the house before she made it to the porch.

She rushed into the house and upstairs. When she reached the landing, Eli was stepping out of Hannah's room. Liberty searched his face for the news, afraid to actually ask.

"Sleeping like the dead," he whispered. Her expression must have reflected her panic. He held up his hands. "But she's not. Dead, that is."

Her shoulders sagged in relief. "You know, you

could use a better choice of words."

He shrugged. "Probably."

"So, Hannah's safe, then why weren't there—" Panic choked off the words. "If it's not Hannah…"

His gaze dropped from hers. He was thinking the same thing. They hurried to the end of the hall, and Eli kicked the door open.

"Ah, shit."

The room looked like a tornado had come through. Furniture was toppled, knick knacks and lamps broken, strewn all over the floor. The bedding was rumpled. At first, she thought it was empty… then she saw the hand peeking from beneath the blanket.

"Mom!" On shaky legs, she ran to the bed and threw the covers back. Neal's wide eyes stared at the ceiling. His neck was ripped apart. Blood pooled beneath him. Liberty slapped a hand to her mouth and let out a sob. "Oh God!"

Eli stepped beside her and rested his hands on her shoulders. "I'm sorry."

She whirled to him. "Where's my mom?" In a frenzy, she whipped her gaze around the room. A part of her was terrified for her mother, the other part relieved she wasn't here. Since they hadn't found her body, she could still be alive. "Where is she?" Her voice rose to a shriek.

"Shhhh…" Eli wrapped her in his arms and cupped a hand on the back of her head. "We'll find her."

Her body trembled. She wanted to sink into his embrace, pretend she was dreaming. For one crazy moment, she felt protected there, like in his arms was the only safe place on Earth. And if she moved, her world would fall apart. But she couldn't pretend. Neal was dead. Her mother was gone. Her world *was* falling apart.

She pulled away and ran a shaking hand over her face. "They have her. They may have already killed her."

"No. If they wanted to kill her, we'd have found her here."

Her gaze fell on a wrapped gift atop the night stand. She snatched it up, ripped off the paper, and opened the box. Inside was a note taped to a rock; *if you're reading this, she invited us in. See you soon...*

Her knees buckled, and she gripped the nightstand with one hand. She thrust the note toward Eli. "They must have been invited in. Must have pretended to be my friends... dropping off a gift." Sobs tore loose from her throat. "I-I just got her back. And now, she might be..."

He put an index finger to her lips. "Don't. She's not dead." His gray eyes locked onto hers. "I promise. We'll find her."

She had to believe. She couldn't lose her mother. A modicum of relief settled over her. She wasn't sure how he would do it, but somehow, she knew Eli would keep his promise. "Yes. We will."

"That's my girl."

"What about Antoine? We should check on him."

"I did. He's sleeping soundly as well."

Liberty frowned. "How did the vampires do all this without waking Hannah and Antoine?"

Eli tightened his jaw. "I'm guessing they mesmerized them into a deep sleep. At least they didn't choose more violent means."

"Thank God for that. So, when do we go?"

"We only have a few hours of darkness left this morning, so it will have to be tonight. But, *we* don't go. I go. You will stay here like a good girl."

She was shaking her head before he'd finished speaking. "No. No way. I am not staying behind. I am helping my mother."

"If you want to help your mother, you'll stay and let me go where I don't have to divide my attention between looking after you and—"

She cut him off, steeling her voice. "I'm going. With or without you." She crossed her arms and lifted her chin. "Which will it be?"

****

Rupert poured scotch and considered his prey. Danielle Van Helsing was still out. He'd instructed his men not to hurt her. Told them to dose her and knock her out, but he hadn't expected her to stay out this long. She was alive. He could hear her heart beating.

He didn't analyze the reason he didn't want them to hurt her. Eli was wrong. He wasn't in love with her.

He took a drink of his scotch and savored the liquor as it burned down his throat.

She was more valuable alive than dead. That was all. And his men might have been rough and gone too far if he hadn't been so specific.

The weasel boyfriend, however, was an entirely different matter. Rupert had been explicit in his instructions to dispatch with that nuisance. What was Danielle doing with an imbecile like him?

Rupert ambled over to the sofa where she lay, her chest rising and falling with even breaths. Platinum blonde hair showed a few streaks of gray. And while her luminous skin had developed a wrinkle or two, she was still a beautiful woman. A small frown marred her brows. She moaned then shifted.

He held his breath… waiting for her eyes to open.

For her to see him. Would she remember him? No, of course she wouldn't. She didn't even remember her husband. Victor Van Helsing had made sure of that when he'd had his friend, Paul Blackwell, mesmerize her.

Just as well. She would be terrified of Rupert if she remembered. Of course, she would likely hate him anyway, since he'd had her boyfriend killed and her kidnapped.

She'd been happy with Van Helsing, thrilled with the birth of her daughter and, for the most part, she loved the island. But she despised vampires—him in particular. When he first met her—while she'd been vacationing on the island—she didn't know he was a vampire. He'd been instantly smitten by her beauty. Not in love, just attracted. He'd pursued her and they started to become… close. Then, one night, it all went to hell.

Her moan prodded him to the present. He held his breath as her eyes blinked opened.

She frowned and looked around, then slowly rose to a sitting position. Those rich, golden eyes landed on him, and she gasped. "Who are you?" She rubbed a hand over her hair and jumped to her feet. "Where am I? Where's Neal?"

He smiled. "So many questions. Which would you like me to answer first?"

He stepped toward her, and she backed away. "Stay away from me." She glared at him. "Who are you?"

"My name is Rupert Kilbourne. You are a guest in my home for the time being."

"A guest? You kidnapped me. Neal…" A look of horror came over her face. "Oh, God. I remember now. Neal… they, they killed poor Neal." Tears shimmered and fell. Her shoulders shook with sobs. "Oh God, he's dead."

"Now, now." He walked over to her and reached out, but she evaded his touch.

"Don't come near me, or I'll scream. What do you want with me?"

Patience was not one of his virtues. And he'd lost what little he had. "Your questions will be answered in time. For now, I expect you to remain calm and do as I say."

"Liberty? Did you... where's Liberty? Is she okay?"

"Your daughter is fine. As a parent myself, I understand your concern. Like you, I love my child very much."

"Where is she? Is Liberty here?" Her voice rose with each word.

"Shhhh... calm down. Look at me."

She lifted her head, and he captured her gaze. "Listen to me, very carefully."

She nodded.

"You and I knew one another years ago. We were very close. Do you remember? Our romantic walk on the moonlit beach?" That night, he not only planned to make love to her, he was going to feed from her. Taste her delicious, sweet blood, drink it directly from her delectable neck. "We settled on a blanket in the sand. Shared a bottle of wine."

Her dazed eyes remained locked on him. She absorbed every word. He softened his voice and closed the distance between them. "We kissed." Lightly, he ran his finger down her cheek, caressed her silken hair. "You were hesitant at first. But you warmed up to me. You were so... passionate." He'd grazed his lips across the soft flesh of her neck. He'd nearly quivered with excitement, with the thought of piercing her beautiful skin…

Then, the blasted Victor Van Helsing had appeared out of nowhere. Even with Rupert's acute hearing, he'd been so engrossed, so enthralled with Danielle, he hadn't heard him, hadn't smelled him.

Victor had pounced, and they'd fought. At first, Danielle had been terrified for Rupert, had tried to help him. But, in is anger, in his effort to defeat Van Helsing, he'd morphed. His skin tightened, mottled, his eyes burned with red fire, and his fangs shot out. Danielle screamed. Victor had a stake poised over his chest, set to plunge it in, when Eli showed up and knocked Victor off of him. Danielle looked at him with such horror, such revulsion… His desire to thrash Van Helsing fled. He couldn't kill him, and he wanted to get away from the disgust in Danielle's eyes. Her terror.

In the following days, she and Victor began seeing one another, and in no time, they were married. A year later, they had a child. Danielle despised Rupert. They'd had encounters from time to time, and she'd looked at him as though she wanted nothing more than to kill him.

He didn't tell her all of that now. It wouldn't suit his purpose. "For now, I want you to forget what I told you tonight. But one day soon, I'll come to you. I'll tell you more." He would never reveal what had happened between her and Victor. Blackwell did him a favor by wiping away her memories of that son of a bitch. But the rest, what fun it would be to reawaken her memories of him, the passion they'd shared. Liberty would be incensed. He squelched a satisfied chuckle. Gently, he kissed Danielle's lips. She blinked, but didn't return the kiss. No matter. One day soon…

He broke eye contact and with it, the connection mesmerizing her. "I want my son. That is why you're here. Your daughter will come to her senses and help me get my son back with me, where he belongs."

She shook her head. "I don't understand."

He leaned forward, and she drew away, but the wall kept her from going any farther. He stroked his fingers down her soft cheek. "You don't have to understand. You just have to be a good girl, if you want to live."

****

Once the sun set, Eli met Liberty in the woods behind the Van Helsing property.

He closed his eyes and exhaled a deep breath. "You do know that I could travel quicker without you? Maybe get there before he kills your mom?"

She compressed her lips. This again? "I have to be there. He wants something, and he won't kill her, because he knows he won't get what he wants."

"Right. He wants you. That's what he's always wanted." Eli took hold of her arm. "You're planning to turn yourself over to him, aren't you?"

Liberty tried to pull away, but he held on. "We need to go."

"What does he want?"

She jerked loose from his hold and started walking. Eli moved in a flash and blocked her way. "Tell me, Liberty. What does he want?"

She brushed a hand through her hair then looked into his silver eyes and dropped her gaze. "He wants you."

"What are you talking about?"

"The night we found Hannah—Rupert showed up at my house—"

"He what?" Eli's tone was low, full of venom.

Liberty lifted her head. Eli's jaw muscle jumped, and his eyes shot flames. "He showed up right after I got home with Hannah."

"And you didn't tell me?" The words exploded from his mouth like bullets.

"I didn't think it was a good idea."

"Why not?"

"He said he wanted *you*. To come back to the EO's. He wanted me to turn myself over to him. Then, he said you would trade yourself for me."

"Son of a bitch."

"Yeah, I told him you wouldn't. But, he insisted you had feelings for me, and that you would do anything to protect me."

Eli's gaze briefly slid away. "But you refused?"

Liberty nodded.

"Why?"

She huffed out a laugh. "Why didn't I turn myself over to the vicious, psychopathic leader of the EO's?"

"Was it because you didn't think I'd make the sacrifice? That I wouldn't trade myself for you?"

She held his gaze. "No, that's not why. I think you would have."

He narrowed his eyes. "You're right."

Her eyes dropped to his mouth, then back up. She licked her lips. "I just… couldn't. Couldn't put you in that situation."

"And because of that, he took your mother."

Her throat tightened. "Yes."

"So it's because of me that he has her."

"No." She choked out. "It's because of *me*. If I'd done what he wanted, she'd be safe."

Eli stepped closer, his nearness cutting off her

breath. "You should have told me. I could have stopped him."

She let out a strangled laugh. "Yeah, that's what I was afraid of. He said if I told you, you'd come after him and…" She paused, swallowed hard. "And you'd get yourself killed." She blinked back tears. "I couldn't let that happen."

He trailed his fingers down her cheek and slipped a hand behind her neck. "I can take care of myself. You should have told me."

"I know."

He let out a long, slow sigh, then bent his head and touched his lips to hers. He cupped her face in his hands and kissed her deeply. She released a soft moan. She wanted him… now, right here, out in the jungle…

Eli broke the kiss, pushed away, and shoved a hand through his hair. "Dammit."

She blinked, frowning in confusion. "What…? Why did you…?" She let the words die. She was *not* going to beg him to kiss her.

Eli looked past her, and she turned. Ryan broke through the tree line.

She tossed a look at Eli. His mouth twisted with irritation. She blew out a breath. It was probably a good thing. They didn't need to get distracted by one another. Besides, she wasn't sure this thing with Eli was such a great idea. They'd agreed it was the one time. Maybe they should stick to it.

She forced a smile for Ryan. "What are you doing here?"

Ryan glanced at Eli, then back to her. "Eli asked me to come along."

She scowled at Eli. "You wanted him to come

along? Why? I thought humans only got in your way."

Eli shrugged. "In case it gets close to daylight and I have to take off. You won't be alone."

She didn't believe him. They'd be there, and back, before sunrise. Was Eli trying to push her toward Ryan so she'd back off wanting him romantically? She snorted. Like she'd have to have another guy in order to resist his charms. Screw it. If her backing off was what he wanted, that was what he'd get.

She tossed her rucksack over her shoulder. "Let's go."

Chapter 14

Liberty crouched outside the compound gate next to Eli and Ryan. Half a dozen armed guards roamed the area between them and the mansion.

"So, what's the plan?" she whispered.

"Don't have one yet," Eli whispered back. "We have no idea where they're even keeping her."

"We found the captives in the dungeon last time."

Eli's mouth quirked. "I don't think that's where he'd keep your mother."

"Why not?"

"Because, in spite of my father's black, evil soul, he has a soft spot for your mom."

Liberty widened her eyes. "He what?"

"Before she married your father, she dated Rupert."

Liberty gulped back a cry of surprise. Rupert and her mother? She'd actually gone out with him? What the hell had she been thinking? Of course, Rupert was a handsome man. Maybe she hadn't known how evil he was. She shook her head. The crazy part was, her mother had no idea she even knew him, let alone dated him. Had he filled her in on their past? Her heart squeezed. Her mother must be so afraid, so confused. "Uh, why are you just telling me this now?"

Eli shrugged. "I didn't see the point in telling you sooner."

She scowled at Ryan. "Did you know about this?"

He lifted his hands, palms out. "No, no way. Swear."

Liberty believed him. *Ryan* was usually honest with her. It didn't matter. She had other more pressing issues at the moment. She peered through the gate at the sentries roaming the property. "These guards will know where she's being kept. It's just a matter of getting one of them apart from the others and making him tell us."

Eli grunted. "I doubt anything we do would scare them more than what Rupert will do if they tell us."

Liberty chewed on her lower lip. "Just grab a human guard and mesmerize him."

Eli snorted. "Right. I think they're all wearing 'Vampire' and 'Not a Vampire' T-shirts. Should be a breeze."

She huffed out a breath, resisting the urge to stick her tongue out at him. "You don't have to be such an ass. I figured vampires could spot one another."

"Not necessarily. I'm betting most, if not all, of the guards at night are vampires. They would save the humans for the daytime."

"You used to live here. Is that what they did?"

"Not entirely. Sometimes human guards preferred keeping watch at night. But, for the most part, that's the way it worked. Either way, since we can't be sure, mesmerizing is out."

"I have an idea," Ryan whispered. "I know how we can tell if any are human." He pulled a knife from his pocket.

Liberty's pulse raced. "What are you doing?"

"The blood will attract the ones that are vampires and—"

She gasped and shot out a hand to grip his arm. "No! No way."

"Why not?"

"I'm not going to let you take a risk like that."

He pulled loose from her hold. "It's not your call. You don't get to take all the chances." He brushed a strand of hair back from her face and let his hand linger on her cheek. His eyes bore into hers. Warmth seeped through her chilled skin at his touch. "I want to do this. I need to help."

She let out a long breath and swallowed back tears. "But, if something happened to you…"

He surprised her by planting a quick kiss on her lips. "It won't. I promise."

"Awww, you two are just *precious*." Eli's quietly spoken words dripped with sarcasm.

She glanced at him from beneath her lashes, trying to gauge if he was jealous. He'd said he couldn't stand the thought of another guy touching her, hadn't he? But then, that was before he'd slept with her, then blown her off. Maybe she was out of his system and he couldn't care less now.

Irritation surged through her. "Grow up, would you?"

Eli grinned. "Sorry, darlin', this is as grown up as I'll ever be."

Liberty bit back a retort. Now was not the time for verbal sparring.

"Okay, here goes." Ryan rose and retrieved two stakes from his backpack. He slipped them beneath his arm and headed out. When he reached the fence, he sliced the blade along his forearm. Liberty averted her face as blood oozed from the cut.

Low growls rose in the air. She snapped her attention back to the scene unfolding. Four of the six guards vaulted over the fence. They pounced on Ryan with a vengeance. Her heart leapt to her throat.

Eli jumped over the gate and, like a flash, appeared in front of the remaining guards. He grabbed one by the throat and broke his neck. The man slumped to the ground. His friend lifted a gun, but Eli drove his fist into his chest and yanked out his heart with a loud, sucking pop. Liberty choked back bile.

The other guard backed away. "Hey, hey guys!" He shouted to his vampire friends, but they were occupied with Ryan.

Ryan shoved a stake into one of the vampire's chest. He lunged back and sizzled into ash. Liberty aimed her pistol and put a bullet in another's head. He jerked and staggered away from Ryan.

The other vampire had his fangs imbedded in Ryan's neck and sucked greedily. Liberty aimed and pulled the trigger. The shot spun the vampire around. She quickly put two more in the center of his chest.

He fell, sizzled into a smoking pile. The vampire she'd hit had recovered and lunged for her. She lifted her gun. Too late. He was on her.

She struggled against his strength, but he overpowered her. His fangs sank into her neck. Did he not know who she was?

Ryan loomed behind the vampire, a stake poised at his back. The vampire let out a grunt and lurched away. Liberty sat up, pressing a hand to her bleeding neck.

Ryan's stake was still in the air when the vampire let out a keening wail. He tore at his hair, his face, grooving deep gouges in his flesh.

Liberty gagged, but she couldn't move, couldn't look away.

He clawed his chest, and blood spurted beneath his fingers.

Ryan gasped. The vampire's tormented gaze flew to him. Ryan stood statue still, eyes rounded in fascinated horror.

The vampire ripped the stake from Ryan's hand and plunged it into his own heart.

Ryan's face paled. "What the...?" He fell back a step. "What was that?"

Liberty rose shakily to her feet. "I guess you've never seen the effect my blood has on vampires."

He shook his head. "God. That's..." He swallowed loudly. "That's disturbing."

"Yeah."

Eli approached and glanced at the smoldering piles around him. "Nice job. We have our patsy, all primed and ready."

Liberty holstered her Glock. "Good. Let's go, before more guards come."

"I'll go in alone."

She turned to Eli in disbelief. "You'll what?" She shook her head. "No, no, I'm going after my mother."

"The more we argue, the more time we waste."

"Okay, then stop wasting my time, and let's go."

Eli let out a growl of frustration. "Son of a... Fine, come on." He stalked toward the front door. She and Ryan followed.

"We're going in the front?" Liberty asked. "You know there are security cameras. Is this where he'd keep her?"

Eli nodded. "I had our friend disable the cameras. He's inside now, distracting the guards and unlocking the door."

She lifted her brows. "You made him do all that?"

"Mesmerization is a handy little tool."

The door was opened by a tall man with a mop of red hair. She, Eli, and Ryan strolled over the threshold.

"This way," the guy whispered. He started up the stairs, and they followed.

He stopped on the second floor in front of a door halfway down the hall.

Apprehension and excitement filtered through Liberty. Her mother was in that room…

Eli grabbed the knob and shoved with his shoulder, and the door ripped loose from its hinges. He eased it down to the floor as if it were no heavier than a playing card.

A mauve, gauzy canopy shielded a large bed in the center of the room. Her mother lay in the bed, blonde hair spread over a pillow, shoulders rising and falling gently. *Thank God.*

"Mom," Liberty whispered. She placed a gentle hand on her shoulder. "Mom?"

Danielle twitched and blinked sleepily. "Oh my God. Liberty?" She sat up and threw the covers aside, then grabbed Liberty in a tight hug. "You found me. And you're okay. I was so worried."

Liberty held onto her mother. Her heart lifted with relief and joy. "Yes, I'm here. I'm fine."

Eli's low voice interrupted them. "Enough of the reunion, we need to get the hell out of here."

Danielle climbed from the bed and glanced down at the long white nightgown she wore. "Let me get dressed."

"No time," Eli barked. "Grab some shoes. We have to go."

Danielle hesitated only a moment before slipping on a pair of flats that lay on the floor. They headed for the door, Liberty holding tightly to her mother's hand.

They'd taken no more than a few steps down the hallway when Rupert appeared at the top of the staircase. Behind him stood half a dozen guards—vampires, most likely. In his hand, Rupert held the dismembered head of the red-haired human Eli had mesmerized. Danielle screamed. Liberty's stomach roiled, and she tore her gaze away.

Rupert tossed the head aside and stalked to them. Liberty pushed Danielle behind her. Eli stepped in front of her, and Ryan closed in beside him.

Rupert's gaze roamed over them, and he gave a sardonic smile. "Well, I see my prodigal son has returned and brought some friends. Delightful."

Eli jerked his head to the side. "Just get out of our way. We're taking Danielle out of here."

"Oh, I'm afraid I can't allow that." He motioned with a flick of his hand, and the vampires behind him swarmed over them, two on Eli, one on Liberty, and one on Ryan. Liberty fought against the guard's hold, but his super-human strength held her immobile.

Eli elbowed one of the vampires. His grip loosened, and he doubled over with a grunt. Eli yanked a gun from the other guard's belt and aimed it at Rupert. "Let them go. Now."

Rupert gave a quick nod to the vampire holding Liberty. He whipped out a lethal-looking knife and pressed it to her neck. The sharp point bit into her flesh with a sting that made her wince. She held her head back as far as she could, afraid to breathe in case the knife slipped into her.

"Let her go." Eli's voice was a strangled growl. He handed the gun back to the guard. "Let her go," he said more quietly.

Rupert nodded, and the vampire released her. "Now, perhaps you will all be a little more… cooperative, and we can settle this like civilized people."

Liberty bit back a smart ass comment about his not being civilized, nor 'people.' Not only was it lame, she didn't want to annoy him and put her mother in any more danger than she already was.

"Come, let's find a more comfortable place to… chat." Rupert headed to the stairs, and the guards tugged Liberty and the others after him.

From the foyer, Rupert led them into a large study. He strode to a bar that covered half of one end of the room. "Would anyone care for a drink?" He grinned at the silence. "No? Well, if you don't mind, I believe I'll have one. Maybe two." He motioned with his hand and one of the guards left the room.

In seconds, the guard returned, dragging in a young woman wearing a tattered black dress and stilettos. Her short black hair was tinted with lavender. She looked like a college girl who'd been snatched out of the midst of a party. Her eyes were glazed as if she'd been mesmerized.

Liberty's stomach tightened. She closed her eyes. *Please, don't let him…*

At Danielle's cry, Liberty's eyes flew open. Rupert's fangs were buried in the girl's neck. Her weak cry and the pungent scent of blood tainted the air.

Eli tensed beside Liberty. The flesh on his face turned a grayish tint. She knew what that meant… *Hold on, Eli… resist.*

She gripped his hand. He snapped his head toward

her. He seemed not to see her at first, then slowly his expression cleared, and his hand closed around hers. He winked. His eyes offered gentle reassurance, but he couldn't distill her terror. She, Eli, and Ryan were no match for Rupert and his army. There was no way he was going to let her mother go. He might just kill them all, right now, and be done with it. Other than Eli, perhaps, since he was his son. And maybe her mother. He cared for her. And while he couldn't kill a Van Helsing, he could have one of his human guards do it…

She forced her mind away from her negative ruminations.

Rupert lifted his head after a few moments and wiped his mouth with a white linen napkin. He settled the girl on a barstool, then poured amber liquid from a decanter. "So, it seems we have a bit of a conundrum here." He tilted his drink toward Liberty. "You want your mother back. Of course, I can't let her go—" His gaze moved over each one of them, pausing on Eli. "Not without something in return."

Liberty lifted her chin. "Take me."

"No!" Danielle's anguished cry came from behind her.

Liberty reached a hand back to squeeze her mother's.

Rupert nodded slowly. "Hmmm. Interesting proposition. It's true, I have wanted you for some time. Even without the antidote, your blood could come in quite… handy. However, I don't believe you are in a position to bargain. I have you all, at my mercy."

"But that's not what you really want." Eli shrugged loose from the guards and stepped forward. "You want me. Back in the fold, willingly, right?"

Rupert's pewter eyes pierced Eli with an almost paternal expression. "My son, back with me, ruling by my side? Of course that's what I want. But, I have learned I can't force you."

"You don't have to. Let the women go, and I'll stay." Eli shot a look at Ryan. "The Aussie too."

"No!" Liberty's heart raced with panic. "No, you can't stay here, Eli."

He took her hands and looked into her eyes. "Even if it means saving your mother?"

She sniffed back tears. "There has to be another way. I—I'll stay."

He cupped her face. "And how is that any better? We'll still be apart. I couldn't live with the thought of you here, at his mercy." He dipped his head and captured her gaze with his. "This is the only way. You'll have your mother back, safe and sound." He cocked his head toward Ryan. "And you'll have Ryan to help you through. He'll give you some little Kelly-Van Helsing rug rats."

Liberty glanced at Ryan, unable to read the emotion in his dark eyes. She brought her focus back to Eli and tightened her mouth. "It's not funny, Eli."

"No, maybe not. But it's the way it has to be."

Realization dawned. "You… you planned this all along. That's why you wanted Ryan to come. So my mother and I wouldn't be going back alone."

He shrugged. "Maybe."

She slapped her hands on his chest, clenching his shirt in her fists. "Eli, you can't do this. You're not like them. Not anymore."

He narrowed his eyes. "You didn't know me before. You don't know what I'm capable of."

"I do." A sob caught in her throat. "You're capable of kindness, selflessness." She shook her head. "We'll find another way. I'm not letting you go."

"You have to." He removed her hands from his chest and backed away. His expression hardened. "This is where I belong."

"No," she whispered. "You've changed."

His lips twisted. "One of the advantages of being a vampire. If we try really hard, get in touch with our true self, we can turn off our emotions."

"Not you. You feel too deeply. I've seen that in you."

He pursed his lips. "I'll admit. It's not easy. You have to make yourself do something terrible."

She smiled. He *couldn't* do anything terrible. She knew he couldn't. "See? You're sacrificing yourself. For me, for my mother. Even while you're trying to be this horrible person, your true heart, your caring nature, shines through."

He frowned and compressed his lips. "Ironic, isn't it? In order to do something good for you, to give you back your mother, I have to become a monster. I have to do something reprehensible." A cruel grin lifted the corner of his mouth.

He moved quickly, then was back, holding the girl, his arm wrapped around her chest. He cupped her chin and bent her head back.

"Eli! What are you doing?" Surely, just to prove a point, he wouldn't—

Ryan started forward, but Eli punched him in the face, sending him flying back. "I'll take you out, too, Kelly."

"No!" Liberty screamed. "Let her go. You can't do

this."

His eyes touched hers and for a brief second, she saw pain, apology, then, his face morphed. He bent his head and gouged his fangs into the girl's neck. He drank greedily. The girl let out a tiny whimper. Her blue eyes rounded in pain and terror.

Liberty rushed toward them, but before she could cover those few steps, Eli let out a feral growl and ripped the girl's throat out with his teeth. He released her body. It dropped to the carpet with a sickening thud.

Shock froze Liberty. "No," she whimpered. Everyone was screaming.

Ryan dropped to his knees beside the girl. Liberty couldn't do anything but stare at Eli.

Malicious silver eyes latched onto her face. "Now, I'm back."

Liberty wasn't sure if the cry she heard was hers or her mother's, maybe both. Her blood pounded in her ears, and everything around her faded away. Black spots danced in front of her eyes.

As suddenly as her disorientation came, it fled, replaced by rage. Hot fury pumped through her veins.

"You son of a bitch." Her gaze impaled Eli.

He wiped blood from his mouth with the back of his hand and stepped over the girl's limp body.

Liberty fell to her knees next to Ryan. "Here," she panted. "Here, I'll feed her my blood." She jerked a vial from her pocket and uncapped it, brought the blood to the girl's lips. "Drink, please, drink." Liberty poured the liquid into her mouth. It dribbled down the sides of her face.

Ryan tugged gently on her arm. "She's gone, Liberty, I'm sorry."

"No… No, we can help her." She whirled to her mother. Danielle stood trembling, her fingers clasped to her mouth. "Mom, you're a nurse, come help her. We can save her."

"Ryan's, right." Her voice shook, and her teeth chattered audibly. "It's too late."

"Come on." Ryan tugged Liberty gently to her feet and led her toward the door.

Her attention remained firmly on Eli. She wanted to speak, but the stone in her heart stole her ability.

At the door, she jerked loose from Ryan and glared at Eli. "If I ever see you again, I will kill you."

Eli chuckled. All traces of the person she'd known, the gentle lover, the man whose fingers caressed her skin like a treasured jewel—gone. He gave a slight nod of his head. "I look forward to it." He waved a hand toward the door. "Now, go, get out. And you'd better hurry." He glanced at her mother and licked his lips. "I'm still hungry."

****

Liberty stalked across the massive yard, tears blinding her. *Son of a bitch. You rotten, dirty, son of a bitch.* She yanked the pendant from her neck and flung it to the ground. She wanted nothing from him.

"Sweetie?"

Her mother's voice brought her up short. Danielle and Ryan caught up to her.

Liberty briskly wiped tears from her face. "I'm sorry."

Danielle caressed her cheek. "It's okay to cry. I know you must be devastated."

She nodded and brought her gaze to Ryan. He studied her with an unreadable expression. Darkness prevented her from clearly seeing his eyes. Maybe that was good. She didn't want to witness his pain.

He spoke, his voice low, laced with sadness. "When we get back, we need to talk."

She nodded again. At least he was willing to speak to her. She would have to tell him she'd slept with Eli. The thought made her skin crawl. But she had to be honest with Ryan. She dreaded the thought of hurting him. He was good—*truly* good. Someone she could count on. Someone whose friendship she didn't want to lose, even if they weren't together romantically.

Hopefully, he would allow her to explain, and he would at least try to understand, try to forgive her. Although, she wasn't entirely sure she could forgive herself. She wanted to wipe her mind of Eli, of what he'd done, the monster he'd become, but images kept surfacing, and it was all she could do to keep from screaming in rage and frustration.

They headed back, and on the way, Liberty explained everything to her mother—her time with Victor, how Danielle had been mesmerized, that Liberty was the only Van Helsing who could carry on the fight against the vampires. Danielle was shocked and confused, but after her time with Rupert, she had to believe.

Tears rose in her mother's eyes. "I—I can't believe all of that was wiped from my memory. I wish I could remember Victor. I must have loved him very much."

Liberty took her hand. "I believe you did."

Her mother stopped walking and clasped Liberty's hands in both of hers. "How about if I stay?"

Liberty lifted her brows. "Stay? What do you mean?"

"Here with you. On the island. I've been so lonely since you left. Which is probably why I started seeing Neal." Her breath caught. "I'm devastated about his death, but I didn't love him. I just needed someone."

Liberty's heart lifted, then plummeted to her feet. "I would love that more than you know. But, it's too dangerous here. You've seen that for yourself."

"Honey, nothing is dangerous enough to keep me away from my little girl." She drew Liberty into a hug. "If I can't be near you, I might as well be dead. I'm staying."

Liberty caught Ryan's gaze over her mother's shoulder. His dark eyes looked pained, but he offered a small grin. She smiled back and held tightly to her mom. With her family around, and the hope of Ryan's friendship, she could do this. She could recover from what Eli had done. But, she would never forgive him, and she'd told him the truth. If she ever ran into him again, she'd kill him.

A word about the author…

Alicia Dean began writing stories as a child. At age 10, she wrote her first ever romance (featuring a hero who looked just like Elvis Presley, and who shared the name of Elvis' character in the movie, Tickle Me), and she still has the tattered, pencil-written copy. Alicia is from Moore, Oklahoma and now lives in Edmond. She has three grown children and a huge network of supportive friends and family. She writes mostly contemporary suspense and paranormal, but has also written in other genres, including a few vintage historicals.

Other than reading and writing, her passions are Elvis Presley (she almost always works in a mention of him into her stories) and watching (and rewatching) her favorite televisions shows like Ozark, Dexter, Justified, Breaking Bad, Sons of Anarchy, and Vampire Diaries. Some of her favorite authors are Michael Connelly, Dennis Lehane, Stephen King, Lee Child, Lisa Gardner, Ridley Pearson, Joseph Finder, and Jonathan Kellerman…to name a few.

Email: Alicia@AliciaDean.com
Website: http://aliciadean.com/
Blog: http://aliciadean.com/alicias-blog/
Facebook:
https://www.facebook.com/AuthorAliciaDean/
Twitter: @Alicia_Dean_
Instagram: AliciaDeanAuthor

BookBub: https://www.bookbub.com/profile/alicia-dean
Pinterest: https://pinterest.com/aliciamdean/
Goodreads: http://www.goodreads.com/author/show/468339.Alicia_Dean

Thank you for purchasing
this publication of The Wild Rose Press, Inc.

For questions or more information
contact us at
info@thewildrosepress.com.

The Wild Rose Press, Inc.
www.thewildrosepress.com